Thomas N. Stone

Cape Cod Rhymes

Thomas N. Stone

Cape Cod Rhymes

ISBN/EAN: 9783337271237

Printed in Europe, USA, Canada, Australia, Japan

Cover: Foto ©Andreas Hilbeck / pixelio.de

More available books at **www.hansebooks.com**

CAPE COD RHYMES.

BY

T. N. STONE, M. D.

We lift the Pilgrims' war-cry still, —
"For Freedom and for God!"
And wear as proudest title yet, —
"The Sons of Old Cape Cod."

CAMBRIDGE:
Printed at the Riverside Press.
1869.

Dedication.

———◆———

PREFACE.

———◆———

THESE rhymes have been written in the few short intervals of labor allowed to a physician. They are the children of occasion and circumstance, to whom I stand godfather. I have called them rhymes, because I would not have them share the fate of the ravens' young, from the eagles of criticism. To the lovers of Cape Cod I commend them, as rude songs that may waken in them sweeter memories than ever yet found utterance, and thus they may read over again the unwritten poems of childhood, and bring back the days when, in life's early morning, even Cape Cod was beautiful. If the reader would understand the locality of the bridge which was the occasion of the rhyme called "Neptune's Vow," let him take Walling's map of Cape Cod, and he will see running off from the bay shore of Truro, a long low point called Beach Point, reaching almost to the main-land of Provincetown. Across the separating creek, some years since, a long bridge was built. Owing either to worm-eaten piles, or too slender construction, the first bridge was soon swept away. It has since been rebuilt; but from the amount of ice forced against it, the continual wear of the foundations by the tides, and the industry of the worm in its timbers, its fate would probably be that of its predecessor, had not our last legislature voted a liberal sum to dike the point, and thus protect one of the most important harbors on the Atlantic coast.

If the reader has no map, let him lay his right arm on his table, bent at a right angle on itself; and let the thumb be brought to within half an inch of the first joint of the forefinger. Your right arm is Cape Cod; Chatham is your elbow; Highland Light is on the knuckle of your forefinger; a long range of hills, called Mount Gilboa, Ararat, etc., form your forefinger (which is the

Atlantic side) to the first joint, and Provincetown lies below that; Race Point being the extremity of said finger. Your thumb will be Beach Point; the space between your thumb and finger will show the creek and bridge. Above the bridge, say at the second joint of your finger, will be the little cove, formed by the creek nestling at the foot of Mount Ararat, so calm and still that it seems the very spot a sea-nymph would choose for a home. Here was fair Theta's grot. It was a beautiful sheet of water at full tide, on a calm summer's day; but the dike now entirely cuts off Theta's lake from its parent sea —

> And now must Theta ocean roam,
> Sad exile from her ancient home.

CONTENTS.

———◆———

TO THE WANDERERS.

CHILDREN, who have gone from our moth
er's side,
Where lonely she sits by Atlantic's tide,
    Enchanted by its song —
Who are tilling some richer, some kinder soil,
Or in city's mart, 'mid its din and its moil,
    Have joined the workers' throng —

Wherever her wandering children are,
Kindly our mother sends her greetings there
    From out the olden home.
Not as a poet, crowned with honor's green bays,
With no proud song, no smoothly flowing lays,
    Do I, her minstrel, come.

But as was wont on some old festal day,
When rhyming palmer, old and gray,
    Attuned his rustic lyre,

Though rude the song his trembling voice might
    sing,
And the rough touches of his harsh sounding
    string
    Sad lacked rapt genius' fire —

Yet if, perchance, his quivering numbers told
Of noble deeds by Christian champions bold,
    In Holy Land away,
Attent with tearful eye did ladye bright —
With burning heart did then each gallant knight
    List to the old man's lay.

Thus would I to your far-off fireside come,
Singing a rude song of your childhood's home,
    Where'er your feet have strayed :
For surely, that ever is Holy Land,
Be it inland glebe, be it ocean's strand,
    Where childhood's sports were played.

I would sing to you of old Atlantic's roar,
That his breakers still dash upon our shore
    As in your younger day ;

That the pine still grows green on each eastern
hill,
Through its branches the night wind whispers
still
Of the loved ones far away.

That the creek, as of old, through our broad
marshes green,
Where the sedge whistles yet grow, our hills
between,
Flows winding to the bay ;
While the slippery eels hide 'neath its muddy
tide,
To the pond at its head the swift herring now
glide,
As in the by-gone day.

'Neath the sun, o'er the bay, the white foresails
shimmer,
Far up 'mid the clouds the white sea-gulls glim-
mer,
The coots still dive below.

From out the fog yet wails the lonely loon,
And the sea-duck is wheeling his dark platoon,
    The tides still ebb and flow.

The cod still is trailing his silken line,
The speckled backs of our mackerel shine,
    The epicure's dish to grace ;
Fat alderman halibut yet sleeps on the banks,
The finback is playing his wild ocean pranks,
    The lobster doubles the Race.

Then come to your old mother's side once more,
Ye children who have left your native shore,
    With care and labor pale ;
Come sit on her lap, breathe again her sea air,
'Twill thrill you with health, though the doctor's
    care —
    His pills and powders fail.

Have the ashes grown cold on the old hearth-
    stone —
Has its light gone out — look the windows lone,
    Where childhood games were played ?

Is the mother's loved form under the gray sod
    hid ?
Lies the father's broad brow 'neath the coffin lid ?
    Have all from the home spot strayed ?

The hill-side, its white path, and the ocean are
    here,
And the shore you then trod is to memory dear,
    Wherever your lot is cast :
For as the Jew, where'er his altars burned,
Ever in worship, to the temple turned,
    We turn us to the past.

Ye have worshipped your God 'neath the temple
    dome
Where painting and sculpture had found a home,
    With music grandly pealing ;
But come, on your own native strand bend the
    knee,
With heaven's dome above — before you the sea,
    Each Deity revealing.

Ye may have bowed in awe, on the mountain
　　　nude,
Or in the forest glen, whose deep solitude
　　　The foot of trade never trod ;
But come with me, and bow once more,
Where the deep bass tones of the ocean's roar
　　　Will speak to us of God.

Come, when the storm-cloud lowers wild on the
　　　deep,
When the tempest and billow, aroused from their
　　　sleep,
　　　Madly together rave.
When the dark night is light with the white
　　　foam of the sea,
And its Maker, in awfullest majesty,
　　　Seems walking the crested wave.

Come worship thus, and each shall turn again,
To his wonted toil among his fellow-men,
　　　Like the prophet-priest of old :
His soul with awe and reverence fraught,
His face clear shining with noble thought,
　　　Only by great deeds told:

NEPTUNE'S VOW.

A RHYME OF THE SEA.

NEPTUNE'S VOW.

PROLOGUE.

W HO has not bent enraptured o'er the page
    Where glows some picture of that far
  gone age,
When wood-nymphs danced upon the green hill-
  side,
And naiads sported in each river's tide —
When to the sailor, on some placid sea,
Came the low song, of mermaid melody,
Soft as the whispers of the evening breeze,
Strong as the current of the treacherous seas.
True, 'twas a darkened age, where reason's ray
Just gave a twilight dim, for fancy's play.

Still, 'twas an age of Poesy and Song.

Mid its dim twilight noble visions throng.

As we oft sit, at early evening's hour,

To yield ourselves to fancy's witching power,

To trace, amid the firelight's fitful blaze,

The treasured pictures of our early days,

To make the red coals on the hearth-stone tell

The tales that now alone in memory dwell,

And mock us with bright pictures that outlast

The prouder records of the buried past,

Till night's dark shadows on the wainscot play,

To us more welcome than the glare of day —

Thus did the poet of that twilight age,

With fancy's revels fill his glowing page ;

Thus made the woods with nymph and satyr

      throng,

And the sea's murmur breathe the mermaid's

      song.

On heaven's high arch, with night's curtain
    spread,

He drew the heroes of the mighty dead ;

Gave to the Fates that stern, compelling power

That ruled his natal, and his dying hour ;

And, as he dimly 'mid the darkness saw

The steady working of some higher law,

Like the blind wrestler in the ancient fight,

He asked a day-dawn to his inward night,

But asked in vain ; no morning's ruddy ray

Brought to his soul the light of moral day.

That soul in darkness, owned the Power above,

And clothed the phantom with the name of
    Jove.

We smile too often, with contemptuous scorn,

At the grim phantoms of that twilight born ;

So smiles the school-boy, at the snow-clad post,

Which last night's darkness made a sheeted
    ghost ;

Give but the darkness to the wooded glen,

The white-veiled post becomes a ghost again.

Take from our age those rays of light divine,

That now like noonday on our pathway shine,

Bring back the darkness of that by-gone past,

Let its thick veil o'er our bright day be cast,

How soon our souls, blind, groping for the wall,

Would back to earth the ancient phantoms call.

Man owns a rule all earthly powers above:

Banish Jehovah, and he turns to Jove.

CHAPTER I.

NEPTUNE'S PALACE.

KING NEPTUNE holds high festival
   Within his proud and stately hall,
Whose lofty dome and columns rise,
Beyond the ken of mortal eyes,
In ocean's vale, whose depths profound,
Atlantic's cable never found.
There in his palace rich and rare,
With Amphytrite ever fair,
Rich in her wealth of golden hair,
Old ocean's monarch, stern and cold,
His birthday festival doth hold.

A thousand warriors, grim and tall,

Guard, day and night, the outer wall.

A hundred keepers silent wait,

With sword and pike, at inner gate.

Ten thousand vet'rans, ocean born,

At the first blast of Triton's horn,

With ready hand grasp spear and shield,

To meet the coming foe afield ;

For ne'er did ocean's monarch own

Secession from his ancient throne.

Palmetto's brawling flag, I ween,

In Neptune's realms was never seen.

No Moultrie's smould'ring embers told

Weak were his hands the reins to hold.

He meets no foes with fast and prayer,

Who 'gainst his sceptre madly dare

To lift a sword, nor does he wait,

To treat with foemen at his gate ;

For, scarcely have the rebels spoke

The word that old allegiance broke,

Ere Ocean's monarch makes them feel

The keenness of his vet'rans' steel.

To traitor breasts sharp lessons come,

When Neptune bids his guard strike home.

Within the porch, on either side,

Its lofty entrance opens wide,

Where coral tendrils columns twine,

As if they were a sculptured vine ;

And clust'ring pearls each there conceal

One half their beauty, half reveal.

Above the home where Neptune dwells

A marble dome in grandeur swells.

A thousand lamps inwrought with gems,

Richer than earth's proud diadems,

Within that dome their brightness throw,

In rainbow tints, on all below.

So bright their flame, the sailor sees

Its flashes on the midnight seas.

From thousand fathoms down below,

Mid upper waves he marks its glow ;

And, as his bark cuts through the brine,

At stem and stern he sees it shine.

Each panel, in that lofty dome

Far down beneath the ocean's foam,

In penciled beauty, grandly told,

Reveals some scene in days of old —

Some mighty effort — deed sublime —

Of Neptune, in that elder time,

When vain but gloriously he strove

Against the bolts of mighty Jove.

Each mattress on the marble floor

Has too its tale of golden yore.

The canopy, the throne above,

With richer splendors far is wove,

For there, upon each silken fold,

On purple ground, with thread of gold,

Whate'er a poet's fancy caught,

The artist's hand with skill has wrought.

The golden birds inwoven there,

Seem floating in the sunset air.

Each flower that shows its gaudy hue,

Seems wet with early morning's dew.

And as the cloud-like curtain sways,

And on its folds the lamp-light plays,

The woven scenes of early strife

Flash on the sight instinct with life.

Beneath those folds, her lord beside,

In regal beauty, courtly pride,

Fairest amid the virgin bands

Which circle her with golden wands,

On throne of pearl and emerald green,

Reflecting back the curtain's sheen,

Sits Amphytrite — ocean's queen.

Ten thousand years have passed and gone,

Since first she sat that throne upon, —

Since there, the ocean's king beside,

She blushed a timid, trembling bride.

Yet, on that lofty matron brow,

Envy can show no wrinkle now.

Her golden locks, beneath the crown

In waving ringlets flowing down,

Their sunny beauty grandly show

Upon those shoulders, white as snow.

'Neath arching brows, twin orbs of blue,

Outrivaling the ocean's hue,

Shine with a quiet, witching flame,

Passion to kindle, or to tame;

Where sleep the charms, that faithful hold,

Ten thousand years, the sea king bold.

For hers the beauty, hers the power,

To grace, as queen, the festal hour,

Or soothe each angry wave to rest,

That rises in the sea-god's breast.

A thousand virgins, passing fair,

With glowing cheek, and raven hair,

More than all gems her home adorn,

Sisters of Oceanus born.

With golden wand a hundred wait

Each coming guest at inner gate ;

A hundred more the feast prepare ;

A hundred spread the board with care ;

A hundred guard the couch of state ;

A hundred more in chambers wait ;

A hundred touch the sea-shell lyre ;

A hundred form the vocal choir ;

A hundred more in robes of green,

Surround the throne of ocean's queen ;

While twice a hundred sisters more,

Fair devotees to Terpsichore,

With motion's music strive to please

The stern old monarch of the seas.

In chair of state, with gems inwrought,

Diamonds from India's deep mines brought,

Sits ocean's king — not such as he

Who frights the novice on the sea,

And bids him drink the ocean brine

When first across Equator's line,

But now, as when in elder time

He met great Jove in fight sublime.

Though from Olympia's proud heights hurled,

He fell, to rule the ocean world,

That curling lip, and knit brow, still

Wear signet of unbroken will ;

The spirit of that flashing eye,

Would still another contest try —

Would fight the ancient conflict o'er,

And battle for a throne once more.

Those firm-knit limbs of giant mould,

Match well that spirit fierce and bold ;

His massive locks besprent with gray,

O'er his broad shoulders restless play;

One hand, his gentle spouse now clasps,

The other firm his trident grasps.

Woe waits the traitor who may dare

To wrest the sceptre glittering there.

Nor sacred fane, nor grove could hide

The wretch who must such wrath abide.

His Titan guards around the throne,

Now, as of old, his prowess own,

Well proved in many an ancient fray,

Where strength and daring won the day.

But now he yields to gentler power,

For now has come his festal hour ;

He bids his faithful Triton call

His vassals to their master's hall.

As Triton winds his trumpet horn,
Strange music seems of Echo born;
The swelling dome flings back the sound,
From many an arch the notes rebound;
While far and wide the fierce tones sweep,
Through every kingdom of the deep.
But hark! as now the message flies
And Echo in the distance dies,
A sweet wild note comes back again,
Beneath the billows of the main.
Low as the dash of summer's sea,
Comes to the ear that melody.
Now louder swells the choral strain,
As nearer comes a white-robed train.
The sirens of the sea are there,
Bright Nereids with their golden hair;
Grim Titans dance, fair sea-nymphs sing,
In honor of their ocean king.

As through the lofty porch they wend,

And welcome shouts the calm depths rend,

Their leader strikes her sea-shell lyre,

While thus the white-armed vestal choir,

Before the throne, on bended knee,

Pour forth their own sweet melody.

THE MERMAIDS' SONG.

"We come, we come, with music sweet,

The sea-king in his home to greet ;

From where the Hudson swells his tide,

From where the Rhone's sweet waters glide,

From Iceland's cliffs, from Afric's shore,

From where Pacific's billows roar,

We come, we come, a joyous throng,

To greet our king with festal song.

" We've sung each troubling wind to sleep,

Ruffling the calm of upper deep,

And hushed each tiny wave to rest,

That tossed the brooding Halcyon's nest;

In coral chambers laid the brave

Who sank to ocean's quiet grave;

And o'er them breathes the sounding sea

Its grandly rolling symphony.

" From China's streams we've culled sweet flow-
    ers,

We've plucked the rose from Persia's bowers;

We've brought bright gems from Chili's mine,

Rich pearls, that round Antilles shine;

We've robbed the ships that patient wait

The glitt'ring dust at Golden Gate :

All these as gifts, we gladly bring,

Fit tribute to our ocean king."

THE FEAST.

The song is o'er, and waiters lead

To where the royal feast is spread,

While lofty arches loudly ring,

As coming guests salute their king.

The wealth that ocean's caverns hoard,

Glitters in beauty on that board.

Rich, massive plate of golden ore,

That many a royal cypher bore ;

But hoarded wealth, and galleys brave,

In ocean's depths had found a grave.

And goblets shine, whose every gem

Is richer than a diadem.

Well matched the feast which ocean's lord

Has heaped upon that regal board,

Where every sea and every land

Have yielded, at his stern command,

2

Whatever dares a wintry clime,

Whatever buds in summer's time.

The fruits that torrid thirst beguile,

Or make the northern autumn smile,

There blush, mid flowers whose petals fair

Ne'er drank the dews of upper air ;

Their hearts with richest fragrance fraught,

Ne'er from the genial sunlight caught —

But bright in ocean's bowers they glow,

And deck her vales in depths below.

Yet never Tyrian artist knew

So deep a blush, so bright a hue,

Nor such perfume e'er greets the day,

" Drying the dew-drops o'er Cathay,"

As round each guest there rise and fall,

As if poured forth at music's call.

Neptune commands, and waiters fair,

From cellars cool, rich flagons bear —

Flagons that Cæsar's signet wear.

Two thousand years have passed away,

Since on a bright, brown, autumn day,

Italia's maids on Massic's hill,

With clustered grapes their baskets fill.

With kirtled knee, and white arms bare,

And vine-leaves in their sunny hair,

And cheeks that glow 'neath sun's caress,

They bear red harvest to the press.

Two thousand years — rich galleys glide,

At evening hour down Liris' tide,

Deep freighted with Falerna's wine,

Destined for Cæsar's lip divine.

For, on each flagon's mouth is placed

A seal, where Cæsar's sign is traced.

But as they reach the Tyrrhene sea,

There comes a strange, sweet melody —

A sad, wild music, murmured low,

Just heard between the billows' flow ;

And as they list that warbled strain,

Deep sleep creeps o'er each 'wildered brain.

While thus at post the sailors sleep,

Lithe forms are rising from the deep.

Ere from that sleep the sailors wake,

These from the hold each flagon take ;

And now the mouldy flagons tell,

The sea-nymphs did their errand well.

Perished proud Cæsar — Rome is low,

Yet still the well kept wine doth flow,

And in its sparkling bead it bears

Sure witness of its thousand years.

Freely the ruddy wine flows out,

Till mermaid fair, till Titan lout,

With staggering gait or sparkling eye,

Attests its age and purity.

THETA'S COMPLAINT, AND NEPTUNE'S REPLY.

The king has put aside his cup,

And rising now his full length up,

He stands before each courtier's eye

Fit type of ocean majesty.

" Ho! vassals of my realm," cries he,

" Ho! princes of the foaming sea ;

If aught has brought your states alarm,

If human kind has wrought you harm,

Speak now your plaint before my throne,

And mortals shall each sin atone ;

They soon shall learn mine ancient power

Can crush the bantlings of an hour."

Thus speaks the king. On lowly knee,

Sweet Theta, fairest 'neath the sea,

With sunny hair and azure eyes,

Thus to her lord in grief replies :

"Great king ! thine ancient archives tell

Where Theta and her kindred dwell —

Have ever dwelt since from this throne

Thyself didst make that spot our own :

A quiet nook, where waters play,

That ebb and flow from neighboring bay.

And there, at base of sandy hill,

Within her home so calm and still,

Has Theta watched, with smiles or tears,

The changes of ten thousand years.

But sad the havoc mortals make,

By every sea, by every lake.

The trees beneath whose boughs we sat,

With wood-nymphs from Mount Ararat,

Felled by the axe to swell man's pride,

No longer shade our noonday tide.

No longer now, at closing day

Dare we on Moonpond Meadow stray.

Still, while we had the waters clear,

The quiet nook, to us so dear,

We hovered sad around the place,

So long the dwelling of our race.

But now, alas! unresting man

E'en on the stream has laid his ban.

The echoes of his hammers rude

Disturb our home's sweet solitude.

Stout piles are sunk; each gentle wave

In foamy torture finds a grave.

From land to land a bridge is thrown,

Beneath whose arch the billows groan.

Thus has the home decreed by *thee*

Been riven from its parent sea."

Fair Theta weeps, the king's dark eye

Soon flashes back its fierce reply.

Fair Amphytrite strives in vain,

With white arms linked, her lord to chain;

In vain she seeks with love's sweet charm

Fierce passion's rising storm to calm ;

For now the monarch silence breaks,

And thus in thunder tones he speaks : —

" Ho, Triton ! harness swiftest steed,

Quick errand to Æolus speed ;

King of the stormy wind is he,

His home is by Ægea's sea.

Tell him King Neptune asks his aid,

To quell this foolish mortal raid.

When summer's gentle reign is past,

And winter o'er the sea is cast,

Then comes the battle hour, — the spot

Is near by gentle Theta's grot.

There let him send the fiercest blast

That e'er on Neptune's realms he cast.

Ho, Thasus ! swift to northern air,

Your master's urgent message bear.

There, on his lofty glacier throne,

The ice king sits in grandeur lone ;

The glist'ring lights of northern sky

Are but his throne's bright canopy ;

As in the breeze its thick folds sway,

On mortal eyes strange lustres play.

Ask that stern god of frost and snow,

As low before his throne you bow,

Ask him his icy chains to throw

On all the bay that bridge below ;

Ice-bound make every vessel wait,

From Long Point light to Billingsgate ;

And bid each restless wave be still,

From Scorton Neck to Peakèd Hill :

Pile up the ice wall, firm and high,

Far down toward the western sky.

This done, my guards shall take the field,

And make these boasting mortals yield.

By Saturn's beard, they soon shall know

King Neptune is no common foe.

That youthful city midst the sand

Ploughs through my realms to every land.

There's not a sea beneath the skies

But there their starry flag now flies.

Down every stream their vessels glide,

Their keels cut keen through every tide.

From tropic's heat to frigid snows,

No wind across the ocean blows

But breathes for them a favoring gale,

With which to fill their swelling sail.

There's not a whale the salt spray throws,

But hears their shout of 'There she blows.'

On George's shoal, Newfoundland's bank,

My thickest fog they long have drank.

No mack'rel shows his speckled back,

But finds these foemen on his track,

In every bay, by every shore,

From Cape May's surge to cold Chaleur.

Aye, not content with steam's swift speed,

They harness Finback for their steed.

As 'long his lightning track they plough,

The white foam far above their prow,

They smile at timid woman's tears,

At lubber landsmen's boding fears,

And calmly bet, as on they fly,

How many casks the whale will try.

Thus let them speed; the briny wave,

So long their home, so oft their grave,

Shall still its cheering harvest yield

To tillers of the ocean field.

But let them not presumptuous dare

Disturb the home of Theta fair.

Such sacrilegious foes shall know

King Neptune strikes a heavy blow,

When low their puny bridge is spread,

From Hog's bare isle, to Meadow's Head."

Thus Neptune spake — dismissed his court ;

They filled the day with song and sport ;

Then each returned to distant home

Beneath the crested billows' foam.

CHAPTER II.

THE ATTACK.

FAIR summer 's o'er. Stern winter's blast
Far on the bay its chains has cast.
From low Beach Point, to Sandwich shore,
The billows' dash is heard no more.
Ice-bound mid-bay, the vessels ride,
Unmoved by ocean's heaving tide.
From Scorton Neck to Highpole Height,
The bay's broad breast is clothed in white.
And thicker yet the frost is strown
By every blast that's o'er it blown.
Far out to sea the icebergs tell
The frost king 's done his labor well.

'Tis winter eve, and calm and still ;

The sun has fired Gilboa's hill ;

With richest gems each tree was drest,

Ere he had sank mid waves to rest ;

Though 'neath the wave, his calm light still

Gildeth in gladness cloud and hill,

As o'er the soul some sweet smile plays,

That was our joy in other days —

Fringing the clouds of present sadness

With memories of vanished gladness.

One cloud alone, far down the sky,

In dark relief does boding lie.

Silence hangs brooding o'er the bay,

On whose still breast the ice veil lay.

No sound is heard save ocean's moan,

And now and then the ice deep groan.

But 'neath the sea is martial tread,

For there, by mighty Glaucus led,

King Neptune's storming forces come,

Sworn to defend fair Theta's home.

In front, firm treading ocean's sand,

Come Neptune's guard, his Titan band.

Each breast some badge of honor wears;

On shoulders broad each soldier bears

His axe of steel, whose glitt'ring edge

Falls like the lightning's riving wedge.

Behind come, reft of spear and shield,

Vet'rans of many a well-fought field,

By Phorcus led ; with steady pace

They wheel in silence round the Race,

And there, in solid columns form,

Prepared the ice's thick wall to storm,

While slow the cloud steals up the sky,

Where Corus leads their wind ally.

'Tis silent all; yon village still
Securely sleeps beneath the hill;
No sound is there, no labor's light
Glares on the dark'ning noon of night.

Now Triton winds his sounding shell;
Quick on the air its shrill notes tell.
From Peakèd Hills the echoes fly,
From Peakèd Cliff comes back reply.
But scarcely has that blast rung out,
Ere Titans raise their battle shout.
Quick to the ice wall Glaucus springs,
The ice beneath his good axe rings;
In eager haste each Titan speeds,
To follow where brave Glaucus leads.
And now, as when in northern sea,
The ground swell sets the icebergs free
The icy mass heaves to and fro,
Beneath each sturdy Titan's blow.

While from the dark, cloud-covered sky .

Bluff Corus hurls his battle-cry,

And swift and strong the northern blast

Upon the battle-field is cast.

The driven waves, with crested foam,

Swift as white-maned chargers come.

The ice sends forth its thunder crash,

As wind and wave upon it dash.

Old Triton's trumpet echoes far,

The vet'rans charge with wild hurrah,

While from the driving clouds on high

The northern blast shouts back reply;

Till, torn by axe, by wind and tide,

The ice wall opens channel wide,

And dark above the ice veil white,

The fated bridge appears in sight.

"The bridge! the bridge!" from front rings out,

While rearward ranks bear back the shout.

4

" Forward ! " stout Phorcus cheering cries :

Quick through the breach each vet'ran hies,

And each does massive iceberg grasp,

As if he did but pebble clasp ;

Swift round his head it circling whirls,

Then full on bridge the mass he hurls.

As breaks the sedge some winter's morn,

The sturdy piles from bridge are torn ;

The tottering bridge sways to and fro,

Unstayed by beam or pile below.

But now from out his misty cloud,

Mad Hotspur Corus shouts aloud :

" Grant me," he cries, " one zephyr's blow

Upon that cobweb of the foe.

By Jove, had I but sooner known

This was the bridge they boast their own,

I'd brought the gentlest breeze of May,

With which to brush its beams away.

Good northern blast, your mildest blow

Strike on that filmy wraith below,

As often on some summer morn,

You've cleared the mist of dew-drops born."

He speaks, and on his fierce winds dash,

'Gainst beam and plank with thunder crash.

Full on the swaying bridge they strike,

And plank and timber fare alike.

Mid icy fragments rudely thrown,

Far on the shore the wreck is strown ;

In wild confusion all is spread,

From George's Hill to Meadow's Head,

While loud mid hills and valleys far,

Echoes the vet'rans' wild hurrah.

But now is heard on frosty air,

Borne from the home of Theta fair,

Sweet music, hushing wind and sea,

And battle's stern, dark revelry.

The vet'rans rough from contest rest ;

With heads low bowed, with hands on breast,

In steady ranks, subdued and still,

Are ranged beneath the sandy hill.

While, as the sweet tones upward rise,

And reach their ally of the skies,

Bluff Corus bids his fierce winds cease,

And ev'ry war-note 's hushed to peace.

Then rising from her own loved wave,

Fair Theta thus her tribute gave :

"Accept my grateful thanks," says she,

"Stern warriors of the air and sea,

Who at your king's command have come

To rescue Theta's humble home.

Again will now our morning song

Echo these sandy shores along.

Again, the trav'ler on yon hill,

On autumn evening calm and still,

Will stand, and mid the misty haze,

There on my white-robed sisters gaze,

As on these waters calm they dance ;

Though to his 'wildered sight, perchance,

They seem but white gulls in their play,

Which cluster in this quiet bay.

Brave warriors of the sea and air,

Back to your kings our deep thanks bear.

Yon broken bridge and icebergs tell

That ye have done your mission well.

Receive again my thanks — farewell."

The placid waters open wide,

Glad to receive beneath their tide

A form so fair ; one moment more,

A thunder's echo shakes the shore,

As from the strand, and from the sky,

Rings out the shout of victory.

Slowly the Titans, wheeling, turn

From where fair Theta's altars burn.

Their heavy tread shakes earth and sea,

As when in ocean's revelry

The mad waves of Atlantic roar

In echoing thunder on our shore.

They lift again one loud hurrah,

As firm they stand on Wood-end Bar,

Their burnished steel, and helmets bright,

Reflecting back the Race Point light.

Bluff Corus, too, on rare sport bent,

Ere back to Ægea's sea he went,

Jostles the tower of Long Point light,

Till keeper, shudd'ring in his fright,

Upstarting, strives to utter prayer —

The one he owes to mother's care.

But jolly Corus pledges troth

'Twas half a prayer, and half an oath.

So once again a peal he rings,

Then on his steeds a loose rein flings,

And as his chariot sweeps along,

He trolls this rough, light-hearted song.

CORUS'S SONG.

" O where so jolly lads as we,

Who drive the winds o'er land and sea ?

Now on some sunny lake we play,

Anon in beauty's bower we stray ;

There oft we sip sweet nectared bliss,

As pouting lip of belle we kiss.

Loving we press her cheeks so fair,

And leave the rose-bud's blushes there ;

O'er marble brow, o'er neck of snow,

From net unloosed her locks we blow.

And now we fill with fav'ring gale,

Some weary sailor's home-bound sail.

Till down a-lee through mists of night,

He sees the welcome harbor's light.

And then off shore we headlong come,

To drive him from his long-sought home ;

We shout the helmsman hard a-lee,

And turn his prow to the open sea.

" On wintry eve in parlor fair

We peep to see the lassie there ;

Watching the lazy mantel clock,

Waiting to hear a well-known knock.

On outer door we slyly tap ;

' He's come, I know the oft-heard rap.'

With bounding heart, with nimble feet,

She hastes the longed-for kiss to greet.

On chimney top we laughing roar,

To hear her slam that outer door.

For jovial lads indeed are we,

Who drive the winds o'er land and sea.

" But haste my steeds, the hour is late ;

Old chanticleer has woke his mate,

I trow with kindlier words of cheer

Than human husbands snoring here.

The Cynic sure did sland'rous harm

Against this husband kind and warm,

For thus I think the story ran,

' He plucked the bird — and called him *man.*' "

He speaks and gives his steeds the lash ;

Quick o'er Atlantic's waves they dash,

And ere is hushed the parting roar,

They foaming tread Ægea's shore.

At early morn the village woke.

Upward slow curled their breakfast smoke ;

Yet ere the sun had filled the morn,

Sad news upon the air is borne,

A low sad wail, " The bridge is gone."

That broken bridge is long the theme

Of morning talk, of evening dream.

But no wise seer the truth could tell,

Why on that night the good bridge fell.

CHAPTER III.

THE VOW.

WHEN twice a year had silent flown,

Fair Theta bowed before the throne ;

Again, with white hands lifted there,

To ocean's monarch proffered prayer.

" Again," she cries, " my sovereign liege,

Again thy throne I must besiege.

For now these mortals proudly tell,

That they will build their bridge so well,

No ice king's aid, no Titan's blow,

Will make its sturdy arches bow.

And now must Theta ocean roam,

Sad exile from her ancient home."

The angry god from throne upsprings,

Through dome and arch his loud voice rings:

"Ho! Triton, here," outspoke the king,

"Haste, my swiftest chariot bring.

I will to Theta's home repair,

To see what foolish mortals dare."

Soon as he speaks the stern command,

The harnessed horses restive stand;

The king his pearly seat has ta'en,

And Triton gives his horses rein.

Quick to the upper waves they spring,

On crested seas their swift hoofs ring.

As comes to Afric's distant shore

The lone wave with its thunder roar,

So Neptune comes; each foaming steed

By Triton lashed to fiercest speed.

From Nauset lights to Highland Head,

The solid sand-hills shake with dread.

Each village started with affright,

As quaked the trembling earth that night.

And in some grave historian's book

'Tis written how the Cape was shook

By earthquake dread ; how roared the sea,

When Neptune rode thus angrily.

With foaming steeds, with lightning pace,

His chariot wheels around the Race.

On Chatham bars its foam still lay,

When it had dashed within our bay ;

And light-house keepers stood aghast

As by in thunder Neptune passed.

Still knew his steeds no moment's stay,

Till far beyond the opening bay

They panting stood, besprent with foam,

Beside fair Theta's quiet home.

Scarce had the horses touched the strand

Ere Neptune stood upon the sand.

As there he paced with kindling eye

Beneath the star-gemmed wintry sky,

He looked in anger on those piers,

The bridge which woke poor Theta's fears.

"Vain fools!" he cried, "ye think to chain

Like Persia's king, the rolling main.

Know ye, who thus King Neptune mock,

How fared the light on Minot's rock?

Let learned fools pretend to tell

How and Why that light-house fell.

This truth let daring mortals know:

It fell, when Neptune struck the blow;

Fell when the tempest round it whirled,

Fell when my waves were 'gainst it hurled.

The rest must with its keepers sleep,

In the low caverns of the deep.

Mine is the dreaded earthquake's power,

That whelmed fair Lisbon in an hour;

Far 'neath my waves its high walls sank,

In its proud halls my vassals drank.

Think ye the storm-tossed wave will stay

At your command, in yonder bay?

Go, guide finback with silken twine ;

Go wreathe Jove's bolts with garlands fine ;

But dare not Neptune's power to mock,

Till ye can bide the earthquake's shock.

Think not I need an earthquake call

To cause your boasted bridge to fall.

Sink deep in earth your solid frame,

Six, or sixteen, 'tis all the same ;

Build high your arches, — firmly make

Your fenders, where the ice shall break ;

I need but bid the worm to come,

And make your strong-built bridge his home ;

Your deep-sunk piles, struck by decay,

A summer's tide would bear away.

Know ye the hills above your head
Were once the ocean's lowest bed?
The waves that raised them in their play,
Again those hills shall wear away,
And o'er them in their revelry
Shall sport again the billows free."
Thus Neptune spoke, — then bared his head,
The firm shore quaking 'neath his tread.
His locks of gray, far down behind,
Waved in the dark night's low'ring wind,
Like battle banner, old and worn,
By tempest blanched, in conflict torn.
His massive forehead, broad and bare,
Was turned toward the upper air.
The glances of his fierce, dark eye,
Flashed with the lightning's energy.
He spake, and thus in thunder tone
Appealed to high Olympia's throne.

" Hear me, ye gods that o'er me bow,

Olympian brother, *hear me now.*

By Saturn's beard, by Ino's shrine,

By ev'ry fane that's deemed divine

On which avenging gods may call,

King Neptune *vows* yon *bridge shall fall !*

Mid ocean's roar, 'mid tempest crash,

O'er its proud arch my waves shall dash.

Aye, more ; since thus my power is dared,

That long, low beach so often spared,

The restless waves of yonder bay

With current swift shall bear away.

From hill to hill the sea shall spread,

From Mount Gilboa to Highland Head.

From foemen who insult his throne,

Neptune again will wrest his own."

Thus spoke the king, and echoes bore

His thund'ring bass to either shore.

5

He ceased, and Triton turned again

His steeds toward their native main.

Again the earthquake mutt'ring wakes,

Again the shore in terror shakes,

Till 'neath the crested billows' foam

They sink to Neptune's palace home.

Far be the day whose records bear

Fulfillment of the vow he sware ;

Far off that dark, ill-omened morn,

When on the breeze again is borne

That low, sad wail, " *The bridge is gone !*

But still far down the unknown deep

King Neptune's vow his archives keep.

MAN'S VICTORY.

ONE autumn evening calm and chill,

I stood in dream upon a hill,

At whose broad base, in careless play,

The tiny waves from out the bay

Once goaled their race. Behind, the roar

Of ocean's breakers. And before,

That low, sad wail, the bay's soft dash,

Just heard between the breakers' crash.

Above, the moon, like eastern maid

Half-veiled, from out its jealous shade

Smiled sadly on a pool beneath,

Scarce ruffled by the evening breath ;

While every star in upper blue

Shone from that pool in brighter hue,

Which lay a mirror, polished fair,

For hill and strand and upper air.

Beyond the hill, below a bridge,

A dike had raised its sandy ridge,

Which like a sleeping serpent lay

Between the placid pool and bay.

And here, methought, in bygone time
Has Theta sung her ocean rhyme.
But ne'er again shall wave or air
List to the song of Theta fair.
Ne'er shall these stagnant waters know
Great ocean's pulse, its ebb and flow.
And spite of Neptune's vaunting vow,
Man well may boast the vict'ry now.
For vain may wind or wave assay
To bear yon solid mound away
And now, indeed, must Theta roam,
Sad exile from her ancient home.
As thus I mused, upon the strand
Gathered a seeming angel band,
Which, rising from the quiet flood,
Along its edge in silence stood.
And mid them one, with eye so bright,
It seemed a starlit gem of night.

Yet round her brow and face so fair,

Hung like a cloud so sad an air,

I knew the nymph divine must be

Sweet Theta, fairest 'neath the sea.

One hand half veiled her virgin breast,

The other on her harp did rest.

As o'er its strings that hand so white

Moved softly 'neath the moon's pale light,

There rose a low, wild, plaintive strain,

That calmed the air and charmed the main.

Atlantic heard the witching lay,

Low echoed from the list'ning bay,

And his rude breakers ceased their roar,

And crept in silence to the shore.

The pool's small waves stole up to greet

Once more their mistress' snow-white feet.

As gently swelled o'er land and sea

That rippling, warbling melody,

The night wind ceased its murmured moan,

That she might fill the air alone.

With uncouth words we vain essay,

To catch the spirit of that lay,

Which, rising like a cloud of sound,

Filled every nook the bay around ;

And, floating up the starlit air,

Seemed but a holy incense there.

'Twas not the words that greet the ear,

My soul enchanted bent to hear.

But harp-strings breathing forth a wail,

Touched by those fingers, light and pale,

As if the grief they gave a tone

Was not the harper's but their own.

As sometimes, in our autumn days,

While yet the south wind with us stays,

Through creviced wall, o'er silken thread,

It sings a dirge for blossoms dead ;

So through her lips, just clove apart,

Breathed forth a strain untaught by art,

And ere rude words could play their part

You heard the wailings of her heart.

THETA'S FAREWELL.

" Farewell, sweet vestal bower,

Where I have spent

My life's long centuries

In calm content.

" Farewell. In thy loved grot,

I dream no more,

Lulled by the bay's low dash

Along the shore.

" No more your waters feel

Yon pulsing tide.

No more along your shore

My feet may glide.

" Proud man is victor now,

Exile, I stray.

Where'er the cruel Fates

May point the way.

" Farewell to nook and grot,

To hill and dell ;

To haunts for centuries loved,

A long farewell."

Like east wind through our pine wood sighing,

Or whisper of some loved one dying,

On pool and bay, on hill and dell,

The sad sweet notes of that song fell.

Slowly and sadly they turned away,

Treading the billows of the bay

As solid land, and mid the night
Flashed out their fading robes of white,
As fainter grew that last farewell,
O'er waters hushed by music's spell.

Madly toward Atlantic's shore
I turned, where now the breakers roar
With wonted crash. "Where now," I cried,
"O trident-bearer, is thy pride?
Stern ruler of the foaming sea,
Where now thine old divinity?
Of earthquake forces art thou king?
While on thy threat'ning mortals fling
Their utter scorn. Say art thou he
Whom Corinth worshipped by the sea;
Whose ruined temples still proclaim
The ancient honors of thy name,
Linked with the old Isthmean game?

God of fair Libya's golden strand,

Where now has passed that stern command

That lifted islands in thy path,

And whelmed fair cities in thy wrath?

Where now thy anger? where thy broken vow,

The vengeance pledged to Theta, now?

Hath wave rebelled 'gainst thy command?

The trident fallen from thy hand

Palsied by age? or was the theme

Of ancient poets but a dream

Of darkened souls? Speak, if thou be

Still ruler of the boundless sea.

Redeem thine ancient honor now;

Make mortals feel that Neptune's vow

Is not a thing for scorn. That still

The mighty wave obeys his will."

Out from the billows' foam and flame

In thundering bass, there seeming came

A voice that made the billows stay

Their mountain breakers crowned with spray.

And thus rebuked my angry haste,

That prayed for wave or earthquake's waste.

" They well may wait, whose lives have ran

Through all the centuries of man ;

Have seen these sand-hills slowly rise,

From nether deep to upper skies ;

Have watched the forest's foliage green

Usurp the sand-hills' yellow sheen ;

And marked each change in time's long day,

Till forest fell through age's decay,

And hills once green are bare again,

As when they left their native main.

While they, untouched by age or time,

Still revel in immortal prime.

Unknown to them the haste and strife

Which you poor mortals miscall life.

Slow comes immortal vengeance. Slow

But sure, King Neptune's vengeful blow.

Beyond thy short, swift passing day,

His vengeance may its coming stay.

But it will come. Its conscious power

Calmly awaits the destined hour,

When boasting man this truth shall own,

King Neptune can maintain his throne."

The deep tone ceased ; with wonted roar

The breakers dashed upon the shore,

Which trembled 'neath them in affright,

As if an earthquake ruled the night ;

And Theta, with her white-robed choir,

King Neptune and his threatened ire,

Passed like the clouds of night away

Before the coming god of day ;

And all that 's been your rhymester's theme,

Proved but a *cheating classic dream.*

EPILOGUE.

MY dream is past, — for now along our
shore
Neptune asserts his fabled rights no more.
From heathen myths in gratitude we turn
To where the Christian's brighter altars burn;
From twilight shadows, where grim phantoms
play,
To where the sun has brought the golden day.
We leave with joy Olympia's lurid height,
Led by the star to Bethl'hem's holier light;
Yield to the past its warbled mermaid strains,
For angel music breathed o'er Judah's plains.
No stream e'er flowed from famed Castalia's
fount,

Like the sweet waters from the cross-crowned
  mount.

Ne'er Academus taught such truth divine

As thy hills heard, O sacred Palestine!

Old Plato's genius in its highest flight

But caught a ray of that effulgent light

Which dawned o'er earth on that glad, glorious
  morn,

When angels hymned us, that a *Christ was
  born*.

THE SONS OF OLD CAPE COD.

READ AT THE PILGRIM SUPPER GIVEN TO THE
METHODIST EPISCOPAL CONFERENCE, BY THE
CITIZENS OF WELLFLEET, AT THE CLOSE OF
THEIR SESSION, 1868.

Cape Cod 's our mother ; we her sons,

As brothers, greet you here,

And spread upon our festal board,

The Pilgrim's humble cheer.

These shores the Pilgrim's foot first trod ,

These hills and valleys bare

First heard his hymn of grateful praise,

First listed to his prayer.

No nobler souls, no braver hearts
　　E'er beat in knighthood's breast,
Than now, beneath our sterile soil,
　　In hope immortal rest.

Not theirs the blood of battle strife,
　　The soul to madness wrought :
Theirs was the calm self-sacrifice
　　That comes from prayerful thought.

The sky above you is the same
　　As when they trod our shore ;
The blue sea dashes now as when
　　Their shattered bark it bore.

All else is changed : yon setting sun,
　　Purpling the Golden Gate,
Slow sinking in Pacific's wave,
　　Still gilds their broad estate.

'Neath torrid belt, where starry cross
  O'er Mexic's waters shine,
Proud bristling forts and rolling drum
  Proclaim its southern line.

With such brave hearts our mother Cape
  Is still allied in fame:
Shame on the recreant who shall blush
  To own that mother's name!

Read ye the eloquence that flashed
  From Otis' tongue of flame?
Upon each burning word of his
  Our barren hills have claim.

If toward the ermined bench ye turn,
  Where sits enthroned the law,
Where, 'mid its judges, will ye find
  A prouder name than Shaw?

Ye tread with pride your classic halls,
  Their patrons ye revere ;
Yet 'mong the noblest that you read,
  One name is Rich, and dear.

When on his marble bust you gaze,
  Carved with a Grecian's skill,
Remember, though he grace your halls,
  Cape Cod 's his mother still.

A painter skilled replied to one
  Who, envying his gains,
Had asked with what he mixed his tints,
  " With *brains*, good sir, with *brains*."

So our good mother moulds her sons
  Upon her arid plains,
But gathers phosphorus from the sea,
  And with it maketh *brains*.

They're on your prairies' waving plains,
  Quick'ning new towns to life ;
They meet the stormy waves of trade,
  As once, the ocean's strife.

Chicago owns their energy,
  Francisco feels their vim,
Alaska's codfish soon will find
  Cape Cod men after him.

They're chasing whales 'mid Arctic ice,
  They're beating round the Horn,
But not a son 's ashamed to own
  The spot where he was born.

Our mother's sons have borne her name
  To many a distant shore,
Where southern seas their ripples dash,
  Where northern breakers roar.

On China's wall her name is graved ;
  Carved on the pyramids :
You'll find it on Fernandez' rocks,
  Where Crusoe taught his kids.

Her brave ones filled the serried ranks
  When Sherman led the way ;
She baptized them in flood and flame,
  In Mobile's bloody bay.

And in her homes are hoarded yet
  Full many a tear-wet tress,
Of loved ones who will ne'er return
  From out the Wilderness.

At Cedar Creek, when battle's tide
  Was turned by Sheridan,
With eye unquailing, Hamlin rode,
  The foremost in the van.

When Hooker led his gallant men,

   To charge the foe in air,

No foot more firm, no heart more brave,

   Than our own Ryders there.

Her sons are sleeping 'neath the wave

   Of many a bay and river,

Where southern cypress gently droops,

   Where northern aspens quiver.

Ne'er need our mother blush to read

   Her record in the past,

Firm in our country's elder strife,

   And loyal in the last.

Sterile her soil — not hers the grain

   Waving o'er hill and lea :

What matter, while her gallant sons

   Are tillers of the sea?

Free as the wind that round them blows,
　　Like petrels on the wave,
The broad sea is their heritage,
　　Its bosom oft their grave.

We may not mark the loved one's grave,
　　Nor o'er it shed a tear;
But still we hear the requiem grand
　　That swells above their bier.

Keep well thy treasures, mighty sea!
　　Thou art the heaving sod
Beneath which sleep, in guarded rest,
　　The sons of old Cape Cod.

The soil our infant feet first trod,
　　The hills round childhood's home,
Still glow in pictures often scanned,
　　Where'er those feet may roam.

There's richer soil, more verdant hills,

  And prairies waving green ;

Yet still we love the golden sand,

  We love the ocean's sheen.

The grand old hymn Atlantic sings

  To these our native hills,

Have spoiled our ears for mill-stream groans,

  Or dash of mountain rills.

We'd miss, as 'twere, our mother's song —

  The ocean's thund'ring roar ;

And 'mid green fields our souls would pine

  For Cape Cod's sandy shore.

We've rode the wave, in storm and calm,

  From boyhood's days till now ;

Still let us guide our swift-winged craft,

  And not the snail-paced plough.

We leave to you your verdant fields,

Your crops on hill and lea,

Our home is still 'mid Cape Cod sands,

Our farms, the *broad blue sea.*

We lift the Pilgrim's war-cry still,

" For freedom and for God,"

And wear as proudest title yet,

" *The sons of old Cape Cod.*"

THE DREAM OF ISABEL.

'TWAS midnight hour — the old church
    clock
  Had tolled the past day's knell,
Near to a northern vine-clad cot,
  The home of Isabel.

The moonbeams pale, thro' wand'ring clouds
  And leafy curtain creeping,
Fell on the couch where 'mid her curls
  Fair Isabel lay sleeping.

The picture on her virgin breast,
  Which 'neath it rose and fell,
Told the last fond, waking thought
  Of loving Isabel.

She smiles amid her pleasant dreams —
  Those gentle tales of sleep,
Those poems sweet, kind angels bring
  For eyes that wake to weep.

She dreams loved Arthur has returned,
  Ended war's cruel day,
Pressed on her lip one welcome kiss —
  Then fled the dream away.

When morning light, like summer rose,
  Blushed o'er the eastern hill,
And Isabel from dreams awoke,
  That kiss was ling'ring still.

The fight was hot at Gettysburg,
  Bloody the battle fray ;
The foeman pressed his legions fast,
  But not a man gave way —

Where Arthur, proudly in the van,
  Lifted our flag on high,
And met the foe with unblanched cheek,
  And sternly flashing eye.

Back rolled the broken wave of flight,
  When 'gainst our line it dashed ;
There fell the rebels' fiercest blow,
  There cold steel sharply clashed.

The night came down to close the scene,
  To stay the flow of blood —
Came on the foeman in retreat,
  Came on us as we stood.

His comrades, in their weary watch,
  Heard Arthur's low-breathed sigh,
As, grasping still the flag, he lay
  With pale face to the sky.

This was the dying hero's prayer —

On list'ning ear it fell —

"O God, for one more glance on earth,

One kiss of Isabel."

Was it a dream, or was it truth —

Who may the riddle tell ?

Was it a pledge of answered prayer,

That kiss of Isabel ?

O mystery of mysteries,

This wondrous world of ours ;

Beneath, the grass — above, the stars —

Within, unfathomed powers.

FROM SHORE TO SHORE.

I STAND at my chamber window,
  And look o'er the quiet bay,
Whose small waves in the setting sun
  Seem racing, as in play.

I see, far off, the other shore,
  Beyond the waters blue,
The golden of its yellow strand,
  Its wood, of darker hue.

And sometimes, in the gloaming fair,
  There seems a palace tall,
With sunlight on its lofty towers,
  And on its whitened wall.

Now night's dark cloud falls on the bay,

    But still the sunlight streams

Upon that far-off golden strand,

    On wood and palace gleams.

Thus, oft from its curtained windows,

    My soul looks forth to see

If beyond life's sad, dark waters,

    A golden strand may be.

Sometimes, beyond the billows dark,

    It sees a palace fair,

While in the hush of even-tide,

    Sweet music fills the air —

Stealing o'er those mystic waters

    As 'twere a holy psalm ;

Soothing the fevered, fretted heart,

    As by a Sabbath's calm.

And oft the golden sunbeams,

  With a ling'ring, loving light,

Shine from those far-off mansions,

  While earth is veiled in night.

A GOOD ENDING TO A GOOD LIFE.

A T noontide's hour, the good old man
   Laid down to rest ;
But when the noontide hour was past,
They found that he had breathed his last
   With hand on breast.

Call it not death ; "such rounding off
   Of life's probation "
Has not a pain, a fear of death.
'Tis but the flowing out of breath,
   A sweet translation.

A fitting end to such a life,

    That peaceful ran.

His faith saw in the toil and strife,

The sorrows and the joys of life,

    A Father's plan.

He drank of many a bitter cup

    The wormwood there,

Yet ever wore his face a smile,

Where patience sat enthroned the while,

    Strengthened by prayer.

The little lake beside his cot,

    Is like his life ;

Environed by its wooded shore,

It hears afar old ocean's roar,

    When storms are rife —

7

But still its bosom, calm and fair,

    Reflects each ray,

That ofttimes, though the storm is loud,

Through narrow cleft of rifted cloud

    Will find its way.

Farewell, dear friend ; though from life's path

    A smile has gone,

We shed no tear, we only pray

Such peaceful ending to our day,

    When work is done.

THE DEPARTED.

WE say that they have gone, yet who may
tell

How near our sphere the dear departed dwell ;

How many thoughts, far holier than our own,

Are but the fragrance from their Eden blown ;

How many a dream at even-tide may come,

Sweet angel-whispers from their neighb'ring
home ?

When all within, subdued to holy calm,

Feels lifted heavenward by some low-breathed
psalm,

Heard not by outward sense — our earth-stunned
ear,

But which we oft in spirit-depths may hear,

Then earth is lost, its dusty toil and din,

And as the soul in worship bows within,

We feel a holy presence, a spirit power,

And spirit-yearnings for the Sabbath hour.

O'er soul entranced a sacred influence steals,

Each flesh-born passion spirit-fetters feels ;

Calmly the soul asserts immortal birth,

Proudly she treads upon the toys of earth,

Hearing the loved ones from their spirit home

Breathe in low measure the sweet music, *Come.*

THE ANGEL KNIGHTS,

OR

THE INWARD STRIFE.

Romans vii. 23.

WITHIN my breast, as battle plain,
    Two angel knights are striving :
One seeks to bind the spirit free ;
    One, passion's chain is riving.

One, lithe of limb and gentle mould,
    With armor brightly shining ;
One, stout and swart, with armor black,
    And brow of dark divining.

My soul, from out her balcony,
　Looks trembling on the fray;
For well she knows the victor there
　Will rule her future day.

She prays to Christ, the Holy One,
　For succor in the fight —
That He would give his angels charge
　To aid the gentle knight.

And as they strive, my watchful soul
　Alternate prays and sings;
At ev'ry prayer the black knight falls,
　At song, from earth he springs.

And then upon that armor bright
　Quick falls his clashing steel,
Till 'neath his blows of giant strength
　It sees the good knight reel.

When shall this weary strife be o'er?

When shall this warfare cease?

When shall the knight, in armor bright,

Bring to my spirit peace?

O sainted one, whose pen has told

Of powers that war within,

Of spirit striving for the good,

Of flesh that binds to sin —

Has now the contest closed with thee?

No war of doubts or fears?

Are conflicts but a hist'ry read

With joy, though wrought with tears?

Like thee, I struggle with my chain,

Like thee, I lift my prayer,

And sometimes dream this message comes,

Lo, I am with thee there.

TO THE ATLANTIC.

O MIGHTY power, in storm and calm
  Held in the great Creator's palm,
And subject to his will;
Before the vast Infinity
So grandly imaged forth in thee,
  My heart with awe is still.

O wondrous Thought, that ere creation's
  morn,
When chaos was — ere light was born,
  To-day did wisely scan;
And saw, amid that primal night,
As now, beneath the present's light,
  Each need of coming man:

Hollowed thy bed, thou mighty sea!

And made each pearly drop in thee

 A servant of to-day ;

Bearing earth's navies on thy breast,

Or tinting in the golden west

 Each sunset's dying ray :

Thy furrows filled with teeming grain,

That waits not for the early rain,

 Or summer's sun or dew.

Though richest sheaves thine acres yield,

No stubble mars thy harvest field,

 Thy soil is ever new.

Grand is thy voice, deep-sounding sea,

When, clothed in awful majesty

 Of tempests' fiercest wrath,

Thy breakers, with an earthquake's crash,

Against our trembling barriers dash,

To sweep them from thy path.

But oft we hear in summer's time,

When south wind rings its merry chime,

As sultry day declines,

The music of thy billows' moan,

Thy gentler voice, thy tend'rer tone,

Breathe through our whisp'ring pines.

Oft have I sat upon some sandy hill,

When wind was calm, and billows still,

And gazed on thee at rest.

Low at my feet thy waves did play,

While lazily the huge ships lay

Like white gulls on thy breast.

My cradle-song, thou mighty sea,

In far gone years was sung by thee,

When life was just begun.

Breathe over me thy low, sad wail,

When day declines, and strength doth fail,

And life's work well is done.

DEAD UPON THE SHORE.

UPON the smooth and yellow beach,
Above the ebbing billows' reach,
Where Atlantic's breakers roar,
We found him — dead — upon the shore.

In young manhood's prime he lay,
Where the morning's earliest ray
Had kissed his pale cheek o'er and o'er,
In silence lay — upon the shore.

No garment showed a sign or name
To tell us whence the wand'rer came;
We only knew some mother bore
The sailor — dead upon the shore.

Some mother's lip had pressed the brow

That lay in marble coldness now;

Some mother's heart, long years before,

Yearned o'er the dead — upon the shore.

We knew not if a father smiled,

Or frowned in wrath, upon his child;

But this we knew, that she who bore,

Still loved the dead — upon the shore.

From where the tide had drifted him,

Thence tenderly we lifted him,

And to his grave, with tears we bore,

Some mother's son — dead on the shore.

Around some fireside like our own,

We thought the wand'rer once was known,

And loved, by those who'll greet no more

This ocean waif — upon the shore.

TWILIGHT SHADOWS.

I SIT by my study window,
    Watching the big-dropped rain,
That, like the tears of a weeper,
    Courses the darkened pane.

I hear the autumn winds sighing,
    As o'er the summer flown,
And 'mid its pauses, from afar
    I hear the ocean moan —

As if for the wave that was parted
    Long centuries away;
But sobs, as broken-hearted,
    From out the neighboring bay.

The shadows of night are thick'ning
  O'er sandy hill and plain,
And 'mid their darkness, the by-gone
  Comes to my view again.

There 's a patter of little feet
  Out on the wooden walk ;
A thrilling laugh on the night-wind,
  And hum of childish talk.

I see the flash of golden curls,
  Out from the gath'ring gloom ;
I hear the welcome, as of old,
  " Mamma, papa has come."

Then strait in golden radiance,
  As from an open door,
I see the mother's gentle face,
  Love-lighted, as of yore.

I know that sweet voice is silent,

I know those feet are still'd ;

The chair is vacant by my hearth,

The little grave is filled.

Fancy is playing with shadows,

The vision is only seeming ;

And yet, O God, this even-tide,

I thank Thee for the dreaming.

And, child of the sunny ringlets,

Where'er thy footsteps roam,

Some time I shall hear that welcome,

" Mamma, papa has come."

Some time the veil will be lifted,

Some time, the scales will fall,

Some time, both parents and children

Will meet in our Father's hall.

I feel that I was nobler made,
  When Death did crown thy brow :
Once, father to a *child of earth*,
  Father to *angel now*.

And when, as now, I sit and count
  The loves that once were mine,
My soul amid my tears doth say,
  " Father, the jewel 's thine."

I sometimes fear that when I reach
  Thy home, 'mid throngs divine,
I may not know, in angel garb,
  The son that once was mine.

But still I trust the word, that there
  We know as we are known ;
And then I feel 'mid angel bands
  My soul will claim its own.

8

INNER LIFE.

EARTH has no form or phase of strife or
rest,

But finds its semblance in the human breast.

The mountain height, with noble grandeur
fraught,

Is but an emblem of its Maker's thought ;

Within whose mind for centuries lay the plan

That formed the atom, and embraced the man.

Each work of art is but a thought exprest,

That had its birth in some inventive breast.

Each breast 's a world, that 's filled with peace
or strife,

And has some outgrowth in external life.

One is a noisy mart, where are displayed

The wares and cunning of a busy trade.

No Sabbath's rest breaks on its constant din,

No sacred silence ever reigns within;

The soul is fretted by unceasing toil,

And life is fevered with its harsh turmoil.

One is a mountain, bare and cold and high,

Which shines resplendent in the upper sky.

But on its rocky heights, no flow'rets spring;

Upon its peaks no summer warblers sing.

We, in the vale, admire the morning's glow

Upon its top, while all is dark below.

But who would leave the fruitful mead and
    plain,

The mountain peaks their glitt'ring ice to gain?

One has its emblem in some forest glen,

With ways untrod by feet of busy men;

Calm in the sunlight that lovingly lingers

To ope the wild flowers with gentle fingers,

Which breathe their incense on the soft, still
air,
Rising to Heaven as unuttered prayer ;
While sacred Silence, in her calmest mood,
Reigns in this temple of the inner wood.
Most happy they who in our world so rude
Keep in their breast some sacred solitude,
Some silent chamber, some quiet, calm retreat,
With spirit converse, and with worship sweet ;
An inner court — by Gentile foot ne'er trod,
Where hangs the veil, where rests the ark of
God ;
Whither the soul, tired with the outward strife,
Turns to the calmness of an inner life ;
From whence it comes with holy love imbued,
Again to toil, each high resolve renewed.
These are the souls that walk our faithless
earth,
With sweet assurance of immortal birth ;

Strong with an inward strength, when outward
    fails,

Firm with an anchored hope, when storm assails.

Their spirit converse makes their faces shine

Like the old prophet's, from the mount divine.

Heaven is to them no distant, unknown clime —

They hear its music 'mid the toils of time.

THE BELLS OF VICTORY.

I. NIGHT.

R ING out, ye bells, an anthem clear,
    Beneath our Northern sky,
And let each loyal heart drink in
    The joy of victory.

Sadly we watched, with straining eye,
    While long, dark hours crept on,
And asked the watchmen on their towers,
    "What sign of coming dawn?"

We heard no answer 'mid the night,
    But the dread cannon's boom ;
We saw naught save the battle-flash,
    That left but deeper gloom.

"Yield ye the contest!" faint hearts cried,

"O let the rebels go!"

From river and from wilderness

Came back stern answer, "No!"

From Lookout's fiery mountain,

Each true heart caught new glow,

And with ballot, or with bullet,

Hurled back its answer, "No!"

Not while our honored Pilgrim Sires

Sleep stern on Plymouth's hill;

Not while old Bunker's granite shaft

Tells of its heroes still.

The clear air of our Northern sky,

The bright blue of our sea,

Would scorn to nurse such coward sons,

Traitors to liberty!

Let craven cowards talk of peace,
Let trembling lips grow pale,
A sterner strife, — a darker night
Shall try *us* ere we fail.

Now is the struggle for the right,
Her battle-hour is now ;
And if we fail, a traitor's shame
Will stamp each blanching brow.

Fail, and Freedom's sun goes back
Upon the dial's face ;
Fail, and the future's fettered slave
Will curse our coward race.

We *dare* not *fail*, though patriot graves
Should dot each vale and mountain ;
Not if our best and bravest blood
Should tinge each hill-side fountain.

The sky is full of witnesses,

If we may stand or bow,

The spirits of our country's *then*,

Bend o'er the fateful *now*.

Peace when the rebel foe shall yield,

Peace when the victory's won ;

Peace when the dark curse is removed,

Peace when our country's one.

Till then we quench no patriot flame

That on our altar glows ;

Till then we grant no hollow truce

To Freedom's treach'rous foes.

Till then we stand on Freedom's soil,

Above our fathers' graves ;

And by their blood-stained altars swear

Our sons shall ne'er be slaves.

Yet still the night moved sadly on,

Dark hours grew darker still,

As if to try the might of faith,

The strength of human will.

II. DAWNING.

But then brave Thomas' gray hairs gleamed

Like white plume of Navarre;

As 'gainst the braggart rebel chief

He hurled the bolts of war.

And then, around the southern cross

We caught our bright stars' shine,

As prairies trembled 'neath the tread

Of Sherman's battle line.

O'er Fisher's fort stern Porter's bombs

Flash on the midnight air;

We hear brave Terry's onward shout,

    Hurrah! our flag waves there.

Ho! tried army of Potomac!

    Ye 've waited long and well ;

Now for a day of glorious deeds,

    That Fame may proudly tell.

Hark! the bugle call is sounding ;

    The carbines lead the van,

The rebels know well, to their cost,

    How rides brave Sheridan.

Full many a steed may stumble,

    Full many a plume go down,

But still our starry flag shall float

    Above yon rebel town.

Hurrah! their line is breaking fast,

The rebel vet'rans flee,

While 'gainst them dash our squadrons,

Like mad waves from the sea.

Now, Davis, leave thy church and prayer,

Quick, mount thy battle steed,

For never, sure, did failing cause

Of warriors have more need.

Fling out thy banner to the breeze,

Charge midst the bloody fray,

And let thy pennon's lone star be

The battle's guide to-day.

Go, lead thy thinned and broken ranks,

Back to the field — to die.

For where the cause is stricken down,

There should its leader lie.

What! fleeing, thou dastard chieftain!

Thou base, ignoble slave!

Hast thou not courage left to fill

A soldier's honored grave?

Aye, fly with thy hoarded treasure;

I see thine old renown

In the darkness of a murky night

Like meteor go down.

Go, mark the smouldering cities,

The hearth-stones desolate;

Go meet the curses, dark and deep,

That on thy future wait.

A thousand cry for vengeance,
　　Murdered in Libby's dens ;
Ten thousand more shall haunt thy steps,
　　From Georgia's slaughter pens.

" Thy work ! " each ruined home shall cry ;
" Thy work ! " each soldier's grave,
That still shall meet thy coward flight,
　　E'en to the southern wave.

Hide not thy shame 'neath woman's garb,
　　Too palpable the lie ;
For woman, when her fame is lost,
　　Has courage still to die.

O chivalry ! whose proud sign once,
　　Was spears and coats of mail,

The future on thy bars must paint
A petticoat and pail!

Cervantes with his trenchant wit,
  Did ne'er thy name profane,
Like Davis with his night-cap on,
  His waterproof and cane.

Down by the cross-roads bury him,
  Beneath some cypress lone,
And on its rough trunk write but this,
  " The fallen — sex unknown."

III. VICTORY.

Ring out in gladdest chimes, ye bells,
  The anthem of the free ;
Fling from the mountain to the main
  The note of victory.

Across the prairies roll the chime,

Along savannas low,

Till Maximilian hears the sound,

In down-trod Mexico.

Bear it, ye west winds, o'er the main,

That Hungary may rise again,

And Poland yet be free ;

And heaven may hear the glad refrain,

Rise in full chorus from the plain

Of sunny Italy.

Slow paced the ages ; yet they come

With days of reck'ning, days of doom,

To those who tread on man.

Fair Freedom has her centuries yet,

Before her radiant sun shall set,

And slavery — her span.

A Te Deum laudamus ring

  From out each steepled height,

To Him who 'mid our darkness

  Did say, " Let there be light."

And straight the hill-tops reddened

  With blush of coming morn,

As when of old, from chaos dark,

  Earth's primal day was born.

Gently, in saddened cadence, bells,

  The brave ones' requiem ring ;

O'er hill and valley where they sleep,

  Your softest music fling.

Gently, for still the bleeding heart

  Will for the fallen yearn,

E'en though their names we proudly read

  Deep graved on glory's urn.

9

Gently, for lo! the altar 's crowned

With costly sacrifice;

The pride of many a Northern home,

In Southern grave now lies.

And many a Northern maiden

Seeks vainly through her tears,

A manly form, a watched-for smile,

'Mid home-bound volunteers.

The treasured lock of golden hair,

Which she as troth-plight gave,

Lies mould'ring on her lover's breast,

In far-off prairie grave.

Joy in our nation's capitol —

From off its swelling dome

The statue of fair Freedom sees

An undivided home.

Ho! pilot of the ship of state,

   Never in courage failing,

'Mid broken spars, and riven sails,

   And stout hearts round thee quailing —

Joy thee, for now the haven's won,

   Through deeds of noble daring,

By stalwart men who trod her deck,

   And God above her, caring.

IV. REQUIEM.

O toll ye bells — a death knell toll,

Ye muffled drums, the dead march roll,

   Over a nation's sorrow.

But yester-morn our sky was clear ;

Its evening gave no sign of fear,

   Of such a sad to-morrow.

Then was our chief all kings above,

Throned in a loyal people's love;

    His was unsceptered power :

But now a corse! so cold and stark!

Those pallid cheeks and closed lips mark

    The changes of an hour!

O nation, sore reft and saddened,

Just as the morn of peace had gladdened

    War's long and fearful night ;

Just as the sweet spring-time flowers

Had budded 'neath sun and showers —

    Then came the chilling blight.

Around his coffin weeping bow,

Ye bear the grief of orphans now,

    For you the hero died ;

In all your land by oceans bound,

No truer, nobler heart is found,

    No gentler, safer guide.

Ye warriors, who in battle strife

For country oft have perilled life,

    Gather around his bier.

In patient courage that outran

The cautious fears of common man,

    He was your noble peer.

Ye sages of the olden days,

Whose wisdom lives in lofty lays,

    Make for another, room.

For he our sage, our leader-friend,

In whom we saw those titles blend,

    Comes through a martyr's tomb.

Lovers of country and her fame,

Whate'er your rank, whate'er your name,

Gaze on the martyr's brow ;

A heart that loved all — friend or foe,

That shared its country's weal or woe,

Lies in the coffin now.

Come, Afric's sons, despised and dark,

Who long have borne the Helot's mark,

With sad and tearful eyes ;

For now, all dabbled in his gore,

Like Him who once the great cross bore,

Your earthly saviour lies.

O South ! a rebel in thy pride,

To thine own glory suicide,

Here shed repentant tear ;

Thy friend, in all thy maddest hour,

With mercy ever swaying power,

By thine own hand, lies here.

Say not 'twas Fate's decree — e'en now

Lay thy red hand upon that brow,

    The wound afresh will bleed ;

Pale lips as if with word divine

Telling the fearful plot was thine,

    And *thine the bloody deed !*

Amid the ruins of thy state,

Niobe sad and desolate,

    Go sadly sit thee down ;

The act that brought war's burning brand,

That lit its flames within thy land,

    Was madness all thine own.

In pampered pride thou asked a throne,

Beneath which, as a corner-stone,

    Groaned ever fettered slaves.

To thy proud prayer, stern answer came

In war's dread terror, battle's flame,
And children's bloody graves.

In that stern answer, read with awe
The mighty force of higher law,
   Nations to bless or blight;
That ever 'mid this world of wrong,
Sweeps calmly on, with current strong,
   God's swelling tide of right.

Chieftain! thy noble mission 's done,
Well has thine earthly race been run,
   We leave thee with thy God.
Our's was the hateful, nurtured sin,
Fest'ring the nation's heart within;
   To us remains the rod.

For thee 'twas triumph thus to die,
To lay, 'mid shouts of victory,

Thy heavy armor down ;

Like warrior when the combat 's done,

Like racer when the goal is won,

Thy brow now wears the crown.

V. FINALE.

Ring out, ye bells, our sadness !

Ring in our nation's gladness

From hill and lea ;

Ring ! for the chain is broken,

Ring ! for the word is spoken,

That makes all free.

Proudly our nation now

May lift her unstained brow,

Toward the sky ;

For 'mid her birthday joy,

Will rise no sad alloy

Of bondmen's sigh.

Ring out our curse and shame,

Ring in our future fame,

True jubilee ;

Our flag still waves in light,

While every star shines bright,

O'er country free.

RHYME OF THE ANCIENT FISHERMAN.

W HERE 'twixt the ocean and the bay
    Our native sandhills smile,
Long lived an ancient fisherman,
    Who cruised the rough Belisle.

Woe waited on the wandering whale
    Whose spout caught 'Zekiel's glance,
For certain death was in his wake
    When 'Zekiel hurled his lance.

More Tell-ing blows were never struck
    By Ulrich's mountain pile,
Than crashed thro' blubber and thro' brain
    When 'Zekiel struck for — ile.

No "*cis Athenas*" 'Zekiel sung,

In time of war or peace,

Yet when he bared his glittering blade,

His heart would yearn for — grease.

He loved to see the foaming brine

Stand o'er the gunwale high,

And when the monster showed a " red,"

Then sparkled 'Zekiel's eye.

A brother had this fisherman,

A stalwart brother he,

Who was his mate in many a watch

And fray, by land and sea.

And little, sure, did 'Zekiel reck

If fray went foul or fair ;

He always thought he'd help enough,

If *brother Gid.* was there.

Once on a stormy sea, by night,

    Before a fierce gale driven,

The captain saw, with blanching cheek,

    The halliard block was riven.

The loosed sail slatting in the gale,

    By every wind was torn ;

The little bark, all steerage lost,

    On the tempest's wing was borne.

The captain looked, with quiv'ring lip,

    Up each unratlined shroud,

Through which, in tempest's fiercest wrath,

    The storm was shrieking loud.

He looked upon the riven block,

    Then on his stalwart men,

Then, with a dark, despairing look,

    He paced the deck again.

" Where," cried the captain, 'mid the night,
    " Where are the sailors brave
Who now will reeve yon riven block,
    And thus our good craft save ? "

Out spoke the ancient fisherman,
    That man of stalwart form :
" Did ever mortal do such deed,
    In such a night and storm?"

"It has been done, though risk is great,"
    The captain made reply.
Out spoke that ancient fisherman,
    " Then so can Gid. and I."

The mast was clomb, the block was rove,
    Rove by those brothers brave,
And then the little bark and crew
    Safe stemmed the wind and wave.

Ho! sailor, on life's stormy sea,

    Oft by the tempest driven,

Take 'Zekiel's motto to your heart,

    When sail or block is riven.

Hast thou no brother's stalwart arm

    On whose stout aid to bid?

Just let me whisper in your ear,

    A wife 's as good as Gid.

Change then the word, but keep the note

    Of 'Zekiel's bold reply,

And say, What mortal 's borne or done,

    That same can wife and I.

THE PILGRIM'S POT OF CLAMS.

DARK was the wintry sky above,
  Bare was the forest round,
When first the Pilgrim's weary foot
  Hallowed our native ground.

Through leafless trees the cold wind howled
  And piled the sleet and snow;
Above, he saw no smiling sky,
  No fruit or flower below.

Clamo Tibi — he lifted prayer,
  "Father, to Thee I cry,"
When straight from Plymouth flats there came
  A low and liquid sigh.

It told not to his wakened ear
Of sturdy bulls or rams,
But whispered in his hour of need,
" The shore is full of clams."

Down to the shore the Pilgrim hies,
With basket and with hoe,
And, as he turns the golden sand,
He shouts again, " Clam-O ! "

And ofttimes in that winter drear
Between his fireside jambs,
With cheering odor, music sweet,
Simmered his pot of clams.

Clams kept wan Famine from his door ;
Clams fed the Pilgrim band ;
Clams saved the noble seed that fills
The plains of our broad land.

10

Then let Italia boast her wine,

The torrid isles their yams ;

Cape Cod still bears upon her shield,

The Pilgrim's Pot of Clams.

Pleuro-pneumonia takes our beef,

Trichina spoils our hams,

But still there's health and strength within

The Pilgrim's Pot of Clams.

WHEN TOMMY DIED.

D ARK was the night, and cold, and drear,
  As if it felt death's chilling fear ;
Slow fell the large, round drops of rain
On our low roof and window pane,
> When Tommy died.

Low moaned the wind, as knell it tolled,
Or muffled drum a dead march rolled ;
Hushed was the room, for Sorrow there
In silence did her burden bear,
> When Tommy died.

Close by his cot a mourner stood,
All mother she, save tie of blood ;

Weeping, she asked, in wrestling prayer,

For *life* to one so loved, so fair,

When Tommy died.

Near the white throne a mother stood,

His mother she, by *right of blood;*

Her harp its golden music stayed,

With yearning heart, for *death she* prayed,

When Tommy died.

Death for *her child* — a mother's love

Still ling'ring, 'mid the bliss above.

That prayer was heard: ere morning smiled

An angel form enrobed the child,

And Tommy died.

As now her harp that mother takes,

New music from its strings she wakes ;

So sweet the strain, so bright the song,

New pleasure thrills the list'ning throng,

    Since Tommy died.

And often now, on some calm eve,

As Faith and Fancy visions weave,

With ears attent, and eyes grown dim,

Methinks I catch that joyous hymn

    Since Tommy died !

THE FISHER'S WIDOW.

H E comes not yet, though I have watched
and waited
To see his good craft's sail,
Hastening, like some wanderer belated,
After that fearful gale.

Sweet Spring-time, with her changing sun and
showers,
Smiled as he sailed away;
Now Summer gay, with all her troops of flowers,
Pales 'neath the shortening day.

His darlings, in their low, warm cot-bed nestling,
Dream he'll come to-morrow;

They know not that their mother's heart is
wrestling
With a widow's sorrow.

In my despair, amid the sands and shingle,
I've paced Atlantic's shore;
And in its dashings heard a low wail mingle,
That seemed to say — " No more ! "

No more! O God, beneath whose care and
keeping
Are sailors on the sea,
How oft have I, beside his darlings sleeping,
Wrestled in prayer with Thee !

No more ; no more ! O tell me, moaning billow,
Beneath what wave may rest

That head, which nightly still, in dreams I pil-
    low
Upon this aching breast.

In visions, oft I see his good ship sailing
    Homeward from distant sea ;
And angels whisper to my poor hope failing,
    " He will return to thee."

Let me dream on — fearful will be the waking
    Which all too soon must come ;
That brings conviction to this poor heart break-
    ing,
    And darkness to his home.

TO MY NAMESAKE — THE T.
N. STONE.

NO puny nursling in his mother's arms
   Art thou, who bear'st my name ;
No tott'ring wee thing, full of false alarms
   And love of childish game.

Manhood's full strength came with thine infant
      year;
   Thou tread'st thy path in life
Like fabled giant, with his mighty limbs
   Girded for toil and strife.

A racer with the northern blast, thy foot
   Leaves not a mark behind ;

Fleet as Camilla's o'er the unbent corn,
> And trackless as the wind.

Speed on thy life's great errand, noble craft,
> Mine only link to fame :
And blessings crown those friends, whose par-
> tial love
> Honored my humble name.

That name, scarce known beyond this narrow
> Cape
> Which gave my birth to me,
Is spoken now by men of foreign tongue,
> Beyond the wide, blue sea.

I have no fear that I shall ever blush,
> For any act of thine ;
God help me, namesake, that thy noble flag
> Trail not for deed of mine.

WOMAN'S RULE.

A MEDLEY IN TEN PARTS.

I. PROLOGUE.

WHEN Adam woke in Eden old,
    Sooth, 'twas a lucky day,
With farm all furnished to his hand,
    And no war tax to pay!

The roses budded 'neath his feet,
    The fruit hung ripe o'erhead,
Plenty of dessert for each meal,
    And plenty of room in bed.

But still, 'tis said, old Adam sighed,
    Amid his Eden joys —

Went sighing round his garden fair,
  Like modern grown up boys.

For when at morn he woke from sleep,
  The lark sang to his mate,
And nightingale his song of love
  Poured out at evening late.

He sighed, as 'mong the clust'ring vines
  He heard the ring-doves coo,
Or 'neath the moon the big-eyed owl
  Sing her to-whit, to-whoo.

For ev'ry bird had there his mate,
  And ev'ry beast his bride ;
While he alone at table sat,
  His bed was cold and wide.

His Maker heard at length his sigh,

    And gentle sleep sent o'er him,

And when he woke from slumber deep,

    Miss Eve did blush before him.

Then happy Adam sighed no more,

    As sweet Miss Eve he courted;

He envied now nor beast nor bird,

    That in the garden sported.

How happy had their life ran on,

    But for that female college,

Where Mrs. Adam lessons took,

    Beneath the tree of knowledge.

The tempter cunning tried his art

    On Mrs. Adam fair,

For well he knew whate'er she plucked,

    Her husband soon would share.

Not for her weakness, but her strength,

'Gainst Eve the deed was done ;

Earth groaned in sorrow when she saw

The Malakoff was won.

Thus has it been since Adam fell,

To toil 'mid thorns and dirt,

And sold the joys of Paradise,

For woman — and a shirt.

Old Adam's son cries out, " For shame

To thus yield Paradise ;

And pay for woman's witching love,

Such dark and fearful price.

" Had I been there," he boasting cries —

In steps Eve's fair daughter,

And quiet as a lamb he 's led,

E'en though it be to slaughter.

Man rules the world — that 's aye the text,

  From which our parsons preach ;

And woman man — pray add, good priest,

  If you the truth would teach.

II. WOMAN'S POWER.

Power is the god that 's worshipped o'er the

  earth ;

The love of power gives mightiest action birth.

" Ye'll be as gods ! " thus the false whisper fell,

Its charmèd power the tempter knew full well.

The poisoned thought thrilled through her ev'ry

  nerve —

But once a god, she might no longer serve ;

No helpmeet then — by this one act alone

She'd rise from service to a lordly throne ;

Bestow on Adam as her marriage dower,

The crown of godhead, and its regal power.

They'd rule the kingdoms of this lower earth ;

Gods *by her act*, and not as gods by birth.

Visions of power came crowding on her brain,

Ambition's fire ran coursing in each vein.

Proud dreams of splendor, glory yet unknown,

All glory hers — won by her hand alone.

We proudly tell how calmly we'd withstood :

Eve plucked and ate as all her children would.

Balance of power — this is the fav'rite theme,

The hackneyed subject of each statesman's dream.

Balance of power — this filled Crimean graves

With allied nobles, and with Russian slaves.

Balance of power — this is the word of strife,

'Twixt modern Adam and his Evy wife.

A nameless knight, I haste to woman's side,

There dare the conflict, there the onset bide,

And spite of lances 'gainst my smooth shield
　　　hurled,

Bear on my pennon, *Woman rules the world.*

Have ye listened, 'mid summer's early rain,

To the rustling song of the growing grain ;

The song of progress, the glad song of joy,

As sung by the corn, and spring flow'rets coy ;

While the soft southwest with its gentlest breeze

Breathes low its bass through the green budding

    trees ?

Have ye heard, and thought ye that working

    there

Was the mightiest power of earth and air ?

Like the gentle sun on the growing grain,

Like the soft'ning showers of the summer rain,

All silent but mighty, gentle but strong,

With a quiet step moveth woman along.

No bustle is there ; but like summer sun,

When the eve comes on her labor is done ;

Done by the founts where life's rills are gushing,

Not by the rapids, where torrents are rushing.

III. MOTHER.

'Tis sung St. Leon, of knighthood's time the
 boast,
When youth and beauty wooed his gallant toast,
All proudly raised his brimming beaker up,
Yet, ere he pledged the wine within the cup,
Named her whose love to him surpassèd ev'ry
 other,
And spite of beauty's scorn, he breathed the
 name of mother.

Thus I, a spurless knight, unknown to fame,
Who ne'er has won — who ne'er shall win a name
 By deed of sword or pen,
Amid the garlands of each festive eve,
On highest arch that sacred name would weave,
 Above earth's mighty men.

Our mother! O what gentle memories come

From youth's bright land, its hearth-stone and

    its home,

    At mention of that word!

As from the low tomb of the buried past,

By the deep warning of some angel blast,

    The dead to life were stirred.

I catch the mild gleam of that eye afar,

Like the sweet shining of some evening star,

    Breaking the twilight through ;

I hear that voice speaking through vista long,

As if it came swelling from angel throng,

    " My son, be strong and true."

And it girds my soul for the coming fight ;

I plant my foot firm in the ranks of right,

    For 'tis my mother's call.

Her eye will gleam bright 'mid the battle's fray,

'Twill smile in joy if I win the day,

   'Twill watch me if I fall.

When the rocks were soft long ages agone,

Ere the hard'ning work of time was done,

On their surface smooth its history brief

Was gently impressed by a falling leaf;

The rocks grew hard in long centuries chill,

But the leaf's tiny form is graved there still.

Our hearts grow hard like the earth's dark crust,

With life's selfish care, or gold's yellow rust:

But no frost of age, or world's carking care,

Can efface our mother's sweet image there.

IV. SISTER.

But not alone as mother

   Does fair woman come,

To improve our manners

   And to cheer our home.

Met you a youth in your oft crowded street

With spotless linen, and with manners sweet?

That polished dickey, and that subdued air,

Show the still workings of the subtle fair.

Enter his home, you'll find his sisters there.

Ah, siren sisters — laughing, roguish girls,

With eyes that sparkle, and with sunny curls ;

Who starch our linen, tie our neat cravat,

Brush our best coat, and smooth our Sunday hat ;

Then coax and flatter till you get your way,

And early bend us to fair woman's sway.

As new-fledged birds first tempt the air,

And learn their future prey to snare

Beneath a parent's guide and care,

So from a mother's silent preaching,

Her winning way example teaching,

Ye learn those little wiling arts

That win the game by tempting hearts.

V. COUSIN.

Then comes that broad, enchanted stream,

Boyhood's long bridge of sighs,

When first we learn attraction's power,

From laughing school-girl eyes ;

With new-felt warmth our boyish bosoms glow;

And the vest throbs beside pink calico ;

While some fair cousin, with bewitching smile,

Into love's meshes our poor hearts beguile.

Of all the flames round which like flies we buzz,

There 's none so scorching as a female coz.

She 's not a sister — this your young heart feels,

As o'er your soul her gentle influence steals.

What is she then? Why this sensation queer,

Felt, and felt only, when that cousin 's near?

If in the dance she swings fantastic whirls,

Your heart seems tangled in her flying curls.

Her pouting lip — her rosy cheek you press,

She answers coyly to each light caress.

At length, grown desp'rate 'neath some waning

    moon,

You kneeling ask life's sweetest, richest boon,

That she with you would tread the path of life

Close by your side, a loved and loving wife.

Sudden she starts, and pale as the moonlight,

The wicked siren feigns to faint with fright.

She 's very sorry — but 'twas all in fun ;

She did not dream — she hopes no harm is

    done ;

For she 's your cousin — you her uncle's son.

She'll be your sister, — never, never wed,

Unless, perhaps, she might, your neighbor Fred.

And then she leaves you with your blasted hope,

To take your choice — a river or a rope.

In wild despair you seek the river's side,

To drown your sorrows 'neath its rushing tide.

The bank is reached, the shore is steep and
  bold,
The current's rapid, and the water's cold ;
You still are young to seek the unknown state,
And better thoughts now whisper you to *wait.*
Long days you droop — long nights you wake
  and weep,
Your food untouched — disturbed your scanty
  sleep :
Till mother shrewd brings you to better terms,
*By threat'ning pink root, for she's sure 'tis
  worms.*
And you live on, although the schooling's rough,
For youth is supple, and the heart is tough.
You live to smile, when after years you meet
A toothless matron — once that cousin sweet,
Sunbrown and shriveled, from a toiling life,
With the full quota of John Rogers' wife ;

And wonder how you e'er could seek to wed

The shrill-voiced consort of your neighbor Fred.

VI. THE OLD LOVE — AN INTERLUDE.

The other day, by chance, I met

My boy-love — Mary Jane,

As I went limping down the street,

Stiff with rheumatic pain.

She bowed to me with olden smile,

I gently took her hand ;

Time was forgot ; again she blushed,

The fairest of the land.

" Dearest," was trembling on my lip,

With love my heart grew warm,

Then fired with hatred, as I saw

A young man take her arm.

" Down with your rival ! " fierce love cried ;
　　But ere the deed was done,
She bowing smiled, then proudly said,
　　" Doctor — my eldest son."

Quick fled the cheating dream away,
　　Back came the truth again ;
Back came her shriveled face and form,
　　Back my rheumatic pain.

That yellow forehead once I called
　　An alabaster brow !
Two blushing baldwins then her cheeks,
　　Two puckered russets now.

I waved adieu — they turned away,
　　Proud mother and her clown,
But as they passed I heard her say,
　　" How old the doctor 's grown."

'Tis even so ; 'twas long ago
That perjured oath I swore ;
And now the love I pledged to you,
Is shared by wife and four.

You've listened to another's love,
As once you did to mine,
And now around your ample board
Six olive branches twine.

I wonder if that thread of gold
Is round your finger now,
Or if 'twas broken by the years
That broke our youthful vow.

Those years that stole your youthful blush,
Brought my rheumatic pain ;
"Our ends are shapen," Shakespeare says,
So good-by, Mary Jane.

Gone are the sports of our youthful time,

Gone the fair hopes of our day's fresh prime ;

Gone are the huskings, the first red ear,

And the prize we took with timid fear.

Changed are the times, and changed our flaxen
    hair,

Since we chose partners for the kitchen chair;

Or took the floor at some fair damsel's beck,

And proud with her went marching through
    Quebec ;

Or paid each forfeit with a lengthened kiss,

To find, like Byron, that it rhymed to bliss.

We sigh, " Alas how changed the times since
    then ! "

Now cheeks are bearded — creditors are men.

For spite of homestead laws, or chanc'ry slips,

We love our debts to pay on cheek and lips.

And 'mid our slumbers, still sweet dreams will
    come,

Of bygone journeys to that once loved Rome.

For to our pillow in a colder clime,

Come the bright visions of our summer time.

Who can forget those loving eyes of blue,

Which shone amid rich curls of sunny hue?

Oft 'mid dull lessons, our averted eye

Glanced where they shone, and caught a quick
    reply,

Ere teacher blind could trace our wand'ring
    looks,

And bring us back from those blue eyes to
    books.

Oft have our cheeks burned with a lover's shame,

When on our slate was read that dear one's
    name.

Oft when our tasks were done, and dull school
    out,

While others chased the ball with merry shout,

Bashful we've walked beside that shawl so dear,

From out whose plaid those blue eyes kind
would peer.

O days of boyhood — lassies half divine,

Who then were wont behind school desks to
shine,

Sweet evening walks beneath the kindly moon,

Whose end, though far, came ever all too soon,

Half-stolen kiss, when reached the cottage door,

Thrice-told tales ended, and the bright walk
o'er,

Ye all have fled with boyhood's sunny day!

Fled like its hopes, and like them fled for aye.

The trees are green, beneath whose sacred
shade

In awkward silence with fair Ruth I strayed.

The school-house stands, — the benches yet
remain,

Where I sat winking — where blushed Mary
Jane.

VII. WIFE.

Sweet wedded love, reminder of the hour

When Adam's hand did build his nuptial bower,

Which in the present, as in years gone past,

O'er my life's evening does a sunshine cast,

To thee I owe life's sweetest, holiest joy,

For wedded love has least of sin's alloy.

With willing heart I own that potent sway

That guides our rising — cheers our setting day.

The bride's sweet love is but the new pressed
  wine ;

"Tis passing years that make it half divine.

When on that breast you've leaned your aching head ;

When that loved form has watched beside your
  bed ;

When on your soul, bruised by the world's
  recoil,

Her love has fallen, like the healing oil ;

When years have worn life's currents wide and
  deep,

That now like streamlets from their sources
  leap,

Then may you feel, what pen can ne'er portray,

The mighty power of woman's loving sway.

But dream not, man, that here you rule alone,

You'll find a power is still behind the throne.

That timid fair one, blushing at your side,

Is not your *servant*, but your *equal bride*.

She has her will ; and in some future day

Perhaps you'll honest add, she has her way.

Her loving heart with greater force will draw,

Than the stern mandates of a tyrant's law.

Make not your boast your heart's too firm to

    fear;

Earth's mighty solvent is — *a woman's tear.*

Pardon, pastors, if I suggest when next

You search the Scriptures for a wedding text,

You leave the story of the Moab Ruth,

You oft have quoted from the page of truth ;

Where Ruth, so lovely 'mid her budding years,

And still more lovely for her falling tears,

Vows that where'er Naomi sad may roam,

There Ruth will make her ever changing home :

Then you apply it to the wedded pair —

The groom's Naomi, the bride is Ruth so fair ;

Her home, her gods, her own sweet will ignored,

She bows in service to her nobler lord.

Just read the chapter of Rebekah's sway ;

How Rachel bore her household gods away :

For modern fathers, when the wedding's done,

Returning home oft find its gods are gone;

And should they search, with more than Laban's

    care,

In Rachel's tent, they'd find those gods were

    there,

Though simple Jacob dreams his bride will bow

Before his will, and at *his* altars now.

There's many a captain treads his good ship's

    deck,

Where every sailor waits his will and beck;

Through wind and storm he steers his vessel

    on;

When voyage is o'er — the destined harbor's

    won.

But when he tries the matrimonial sea,

An undercurrent sets his ship alee.

And oft, like Paddy's stubborn bit of pork,

Steering for Dublin, he arrives at Cork.

Man, like the shaft that crowns old Bunker's

Hill,

Amid the raging of the storm is still.

But the tall shaft with gentle motion sways,

As on its sides the bright warm sunbeam plays.

Thus woman's smile, so bright, so warm, so

still,

Bends man's stern nature to her better will.

She guideth most when least she seems to

guide.

'Tis not the power, but how the power 's applied,

That shows true wisdom and mechanic skill,

To move dead matter at its owner's will.

How woman rules, I may not, cannot tell;

She does it gently, and she does it well.

VIII. BACHELOR LIFE.

Say you, " I'll lead a bach'lor's jolly life,

Unvexed by children, and unswayed by wife,

Go where I like, stay when and where I please,

I'll lead a life of free, untrammeled ease.

No woman bends me by her iron thrall,

To do her bidding, wait her every call.

Free as the air that sweeps o'er vale and hill,

I'll own no master but my own strong will."

Go on, good master — learn to live for self,

Steel case your bosom, hoard your paltry pelf;

Go, fool, and strive to dam up nature's tide,

To bend the spirit to your selfish pride.

Like the old king who chained the stormy sea,

Which in its freedom dared his majesty,

You'll find its tide will mock your vain assay,

That nature's waves will break each dam away.

You dare her vengeance, and in gathered wrath,

A dark Nemesis haunts your future path.

Too late, mayhap, you'll learn in years to come,

Without a wife man ne'er can have a home.

'Tis evening hour ; I see you leave the streets :

No smiling wife your homeward footsteps greets,

No children's welcome — no little patt'ring feet,

No " Here 's papa ! " no childish accents sweet,

Shout forth their glee : not these the joys you
hoard,

You have no *home* — you do not *live* — you
board.

On human hearts you have no joyous hold ;

You have no heart love — that 's not bought
with gold.

'Tis but a lusting of your hoarded pelf ;

There is no loving of the *man* himself.

You've banished woman, scorned her loving
    power,
Now comes the terror of her vengeful hour.
No chubby cherub chirrups on your knee,
No smiling wife prepares your toast and tea.
You're served and waited for so much a week ;
The paltry greed is all your waiters seek.
Your unblest room is up a winding stair ;
There stands your bed, with one lone pillow
    there ;
Narrow that bed, type of your coming fate,
Cold is that room, dark the unfilled grate.
Unloved and lone you shivering sink to bed,
Hot brick at feet, and night-cap on your head.
In troubled sleep you dream your bride is fair,
And hug the *pillow* — *for she isn't there.*

IX. A RECIPE FOR MATRIMONIAL BLUES.

My married friend, if in these taxing times

You e'er grow blue, about old Christmas chimes,

And sigh in secret for the days of yore,

Ere you a father's honored title bore,

And knew no duns for such oft-coming dues

As wife's new bonnet, or six children's shoes —

Your house was free from the eternal noise

Of girlish chatter, and of rough hewn boys —

Just let your children and your good wife roam,

One wintry four weeks from your cosy home,

And when they 're off, their noise and chatter

 gone,

Sit by your fire, enjoy yourself *alone.*

How still the house so late all full of glee ;

How burnt the toast, how tasteless is the tea.

A smile has gone that gave the stomach zest,

That oft of old your humblest meal had blest.

Music from out your quiet halls has fled,

The house is sad, as if it mourned the dead.

Your silent dog sits by the hearth alone,

His very tail wags slowly — *all are gone.*

The papered walls take on a leaden hue.

Your faithful mirror shows a face that's blue.

Try it a month, and ere that time has gone

You'll almost swear man ne'er should live
  alone.

And ever after, through your mortal life,

You'll bless the fate that gave you chicks and
  wife.

X. FINALE.

I've heard some cheats in manhood's form

    (Their lip in scorning curled),

Boast that woman's but a slave,

    That man must rule the world.

So have I heard, some summer's morn,

    Old Plato's manlike boaster,

That proud and strutting dunghill fowl

    So aptly termed a *rooster* —

Upon some barnyard perch or pole

    Make hill and valley ring,

With mighty deeds that he had done,

    Like Babylon's foolish king.

He never tells, while he abroad

    'Mong concubines may roam,

Of the quiet hen, whose constant care

    Keeps the white eggs warm at home.

Nor tells he, when the brood is hatched,

    Who finds for them the worm ;

Nor 'neath whose wings they safety seek,

    From threatning hawk or storm.

But there he stands, with open throat,

    To let the wide earth know

That he 's the might monarch *there,*

    All powerful — to crow.

A RHYMSTER'S VISIT TO PARNASSUS

AFTER AN INVITATION FROM A LADIES' ASSOCIA-
TION, TO READ A POEM AT THEIR FESTIVAL.

L ADIES, to me your hon'ring message came,

   As came to Scotia's son the sign of flame,

Stirring anew the frozen blood of age,

To write his name upon his country's page

   In deeds that might not die.

And I resolved, despite recorded vow,

My whit'ning locks, my bald, care-wrinkled brow,

   And courting days gone by,

Yet once again the oft-rejected prayer

To proffer to those proud coquettish fair,

Who haunt the caverns of the Delphic wood,

And guard the fountains of Castalia's flood—

 Those crabbed old maids nine.

I'll not tell how oft o'er rocks I stumbled,

Or before those crones my stiff knees humbled,

 All in those groves of pine.

I begged one draught from out Castalia's fount,

That gushes up within the sacred mount,

One only draught, from that bright crystal flood,

To warm the current of my age-chilled blood,

 And tune my rustic lyre;

That, though no youth, I yet might once again,

On rustic pipe, with some untutored strain,

 To lady's grace aspire.

But all in vain; the stern Melpomene

Turned with proud scorn her haughty glance

 on me:

"Shall I," she cried, "who've ruled for ages
      long,
Without a rival, as the queen of song,
      Who tuned old Homer's lyre —
Shall I, to grace a fleeting festal hour
Grant to a medic this poetic power
      And his dull soul inspire?
Doctor, avaunt!" and proud she strode away,
As if a Juno, on her wedding day.

    Young Terpsichore came dancing by,
    With rosy lip, and roguish eye,
    With buskined foot, and flowing hair,
    And step as light as mountain air.
"What now, gray-beard," she laughing said,
"Art thou a widower, come to wed
    The stern and dark Melpomene,
    Or dance a merry dance with me?"

With tearful eye, and mournful air,

I begged the nymph to hear my prayer.

She listened with the kindest heed,

And promised to fulfill my need.

With zeal she hasted to her task,

And soon returned with well-filled flask ;

" Take this," she said, with wicked air,

" 'Twill warm your blood, or change your hair.'

I held the liquid 'gainst the sky —

No crystal wave, but dingy dye,

Dark as the turbid streams that mix

In the black channel of the Styx.

Then fled the nymph, and from afar

She mocking sung, " Ha, ha ! ha, ha !

The old man came for Castalia's flood,

To warm again his frosty blood ;

I gave, ha, ha ! — with kindest air,

Styx's black dye — for his old gray hair."

And every nymph from woods afar,

Echoed her mocking "Ha ha, ha!"

Mad, from the taunting fair I turned ;

Within my breast hot fever burned ;

Yet thanked the stars that still were there

Maidens more lovely, kind, and fair,

Than *those old maids with flowing hair.*

A RHYMSTER'S DREAM

AFTER A SUPPER AND MEETING TO EXTEND CAPE
COD RAILROAD TO PROVINCETOWN.

SUPPER was o'er, the oysters ate,
  The logic all expended ;
The darkness of our village hall
  Told all " The meeting 's ended."

At midnight I in office sat,
  After that famous day,
What time the dream-god's elfin crew
  Round others' pillows play.

My feet were higher than the spot
  Where brains *sometimes* are found,
And like a " soothing syrup" came
  A sleep both long and sound.

Methought I saw a railroad car
  Come clatt'ring down the Cape,
Drawn by a snorting iron steed,
  Demon of uncouth shape.

Old Cape Cod, like a boggy marsh,
  Shook 'neath his mighty tread ;
Each pine tree, as the demon passed,
  Low bowed its tufted head.

The Three Lights like three glow-worms shone,
  As rushed the monster by ;
The Highland showed but taper dim
  Before his blazing eye.

Each eel in Eastham's famous pond
  Turned white with very fear,
And every quahaug oped his mouth,
  In fright, from ear to ear.

13

A piercing shriek was in my ear,

   As if a war-whoop sounded,

And by, with wildly flying robes,

   A stalwart Indian bounded.

"It comes, it comes!" I heard him cry,

   "The fiend that broke my sleep;

He 's chased me from my prairie land,

   Now let him try the deep."

And as a wail of sharp distress

   Rose on the air of night,

Beneath the wave the flying form

   Swift vanished from my sight.

Still sped the demon on, and still

   Clattered the whirling car,

His mouth a flame — and his lone eye

   Glared on the night afar.

Each oyster off on Wellfleet flats,

  Gasped in his sandy bed,

Each horse-foot ploughing Smalley's bar

  Turned his long tail and fled.

Through Wellfleet village quick he sped,

  Then straight through Truro wood,

For, like a traveller in haste,

  He shunned their county road.

The dogfish heard it off the shore,

  And sought his deep sea bed ;

In vain South Truro sighed for clams,

  For every clam was dead.

He clomb old Truro's highest hills,

  Along her marshes flashed ;

Pond Village started with affright,

  As by in haste he dashed.

Low Beach Point trembled, as he trod
  Upon its sandy ridge,
And like a Titan madly leaped
  Across the tott'ring bridge.

The codfish heard its thund'ring clang,
  And woeful ·cried, " Alas ! "
Each lobster lifted claws in prayer,
  And paled each striped bass.   ·

E'en bluefish left his prey untouched,
  At snorting of that steed ;
And finback cut the foaming wave,
  With more than lightning speed —

While mack'rel off on Middle Bank
  In sullen silence sighed ;
And halibut on Jeffries' Shoal,
  Low bent his head and cried.

" Ah now," they said, " the deed is done,
  The right arm now is free ;
Now can she send her harvest in
  She gathers from the sea.

" No waiting now, for wind or tide,
  No care for storm or sun ;
We only snap at tempting bait —
  'Presto ! their market 's done.

" And we, who sport in ocean's depths
  To-night, as careless fish,
To-morrow's noon sees smoking hot
  On Boston merchant's dish."

I heard a noise in poultry yards ;
  The fowl, with wing and bill,
Were breaking through each slatted coop,
  With all a female's will.

The rooster crowed, as off they sped,

Scorning all detention ;

"What now?" I cried. Rooster replied,

"'Tis a hen convention."

I stood upon a Truro hill,

Looked down her deepest vale,

And saw, from every poultry yard,

Thither each inmate sail.

A turkey proud, with wattles red,

Filled well the speaker's chair,

While on the ground, as caucus scribes,

Scratched fast three pullets fair.

"We've met," the red old speaker said,

"To tell the world our mind

Upon this madness that has seized

Bipeds of human kind.

" We thought that here, on old Cape Cod,

    We were from railroads free,

For here their cars are white-winged cralt,

    Their road the level sea.

" But now, alas! the fever's here ;

    Those squinting engineers,

These railroad suppers, well I think

    May wake our darkest fears."

" Let's put it down," a rooster cried,

    Black as a night with rain

(His grandsire won his golden spurs

    In cockpits of old Spain).

" I'll dare the monster to the fight,

    I'll risk Hidalgo blood ;

And if I in the contest fall,

    'Tis for my kindred's good."

" Outside barbarians," Shanghai said,

" Who 'gainst all poultry sin,

We'll crush them, *as our emp'ror does,*

With flaming bulletin."

Up sprang a hen of native breed

(For female rights was she),

" Poor fools," she cried, " to think to stop

These Yankees by decree.

" Just touch their purse, the heart is there,

That does each effort move ;

'Tis stronger than all votes or prayers,

For 'tis the cash they love.

" Tell them that if this road is laid,

It ne'er shall profits pay,

For ne'er a hen upon Cape Cod,

Another egg will lay.

"It is too much that we must lay
  For Boston and New York ;
Our Yankee eggs shall never fry
  Beside the Dutchman's pork.

"True, it may bring our patriot heads
  Upon the bloody block ;
But ne'er a hen's maternal grief
  Shall they for profit mock."

"That 's it," a female turkey sighed,
  "I've raised full many a brood,
And seen three scores of children fair
  Lie dabbled in their blood."

"Amen !" hissed out an ancient goose,
  "My ancestors saved Rome,
Let's pass the vote, for daylight 's near,
  And goslings wait at home."

They passed the vote, with each wing up,
　　To waken human fears,
And bade the scribes a copy give,
　　To squinting engineers.

But onward passed that demon steed,
　　Wild blazed that lone eye still,
Till like a courser spent it stood
　　At foot of Highpole hill.

I heard a mother chirruping
　　To baby on her knee,
" Papa is now in New York, dear.
　　He'll be at home to tea."

A lassie read a telegram —
　　Thus spoke the mystic wire :
" By night's express I come to you ;
　　Kindle the parlor fire."

"I vow," an old man snarling cried,

    He of the old ox team,

Whose infant slumbers ne'er were broke

    By locomotive scream —

"These pesky railroads will, I fear,

    Soon twitch me off my legs ;

O for the days of calico,

    Which goodwife bought with eggs.

"But now, if daughter wants a gown,

    She'll off like lightning dash

To lunch at Copeland's, *a la mode,*

    At Jordan's spend my cash.

When she returns she 's Frenchified

    Or Dutch for near a week ;

And talks of Coburgs, Bismarck brown,

    Chinchilla, moire antique.

Methought each horse gave up the ghost
   Before that steed of fire;
Higgins no stages drove by day,
   By night no Black Maria.

No packets then did roll and lurch,
   With landsmen paying toll;
No lady crying " Keep her still !
   O steward, hand a bowl."

But easy on their cushioned seats,
   As by their own fireside,
They studied fashions, as they sped
   Along the circling ride.

I heard the shriek of early train
   And started from my chair ;
The railroad vanished, and the steed
   Proved but an oyster-mare.

A HOODLESS SONG OF A SHIRT.

'TIS told in fable — legend strange and old,

    Such as full oft the youthful fancy hold —

That once it happened, in a by-gone time,

Amid the brightness of an Eastern clime,

A Satrap languished in his palace fair —

Its marble halls, its viands rich and rare;

And treasures countless as the yellow sand

That brightly sparkled on its ocean strand.

Vainly did music, with its wizard power,

Woo to his couch one sleep-refreshing hour ;

Vain, in his harem, did the dancing girls,

With tinkling bells, and most luxurious whirls,

Strive to his lip to bring one wonted smile;

He languid gazed, but only sighed the while.

Vainly did Lulu with her thousand charms,

Tempt her old lover to her willing arms;

Vainly the dark Zenoba, lotus-eyed,

Heiress of regal blood and queenly pride,

Sat like a servant at his royal feet,

And sung old ballads, with a voice as sweet

As bulbul warbles to the opening rose,

When morning sun in distant Persia glows.

But all in vain; the Satrap languished still.

At length a prophet, by kind Allah sent,

Thus spoke his message as he lowly bent:

"If our great master should the *shirt* but wear

Be it of silk, or linen fine, or hair,

That decks the man with his own *lot content*,

Whate'er the portion that 's by Allah sent,

Again blest health within his veins would glow,

And joy once more would crown his royal brow."

Throughout the realm the hast'ning message

    sped,

To find the man that to content was wed.

They sought amid the monarch's courtly train,

Asked of each noble there, but asked in vain.

They searched each city, palace, hall, and store

From all came back the cry, "A little more."

Each would be happy, each contented rest,

Were his the lot that had his neighbor blest.

At last, in hut beside a mountain stream,

They found the subject of the prophet's dream

Content, like Horace, with his present store;

He asked not gods above nor men for more.

"Quick, tell me, slave ! " the anxious courtier

    cries,

"Ask you no added wealth from earth or skies ;

No broader farm, no palace for this hut —

Say, has your bliss no lurking if or but?"

"I am content — of Allah ask no more

Than what he gave in this my present store."

"Eureka!" shouts the courtier, "pleasure now

Shall sit again upon my master's brow."

They seized the happy man, and joyous bear

Him back in triumph to the palace fair,

Where languished still the patient unrelieved,

Though all his kingdom o'er his illness grieved.

But hope again glows in the royal breast,

The man is found, *his shirt will do the rest.*

In haste they cast his garments coarse aside,

Each girdling band in eager haste divide ,

To find this truth, 'neath peasant garb and dirt,

" *Joyous contentment never wore a shirt !* "

A SAND-HILL REVERIE.

M Y mother Cape, upon thy soil
      No classic shrines arise ;
No vineyards with the purpling grape,
   As 'neath Italia's skies.

Not thine the groves where Plato taught
   His doctrines half divine ;
No Virgil sung the fate of Troy
   Upon these shores of thine.

Ne'er on these sands did chivalry
   Marshal its mailèd knights ;
No scald or bard enshrined thy name
   Among his Druid rites.

Thine is no name of hero old,

    Renowned in herald lore ;

That humble name no errant knight

    Upon his scutcheon bore.

Thine ancient story who can tell ?

    How long old ocean rolled

Its breakers, with their earthquake shock,

    Upon thy sands of gold —

Who lived amid thy forest shades,

    When, in our father's land,

The Briton with the Roman fought

    Upon its bloody strand —

Who roamed these hills, or built their homes

    Within each shaded dell —

No searcher of Time's mouldy tomes

    Their history may tell.

Where now I stand leviathans have sported,

And pond'rous whales their dusky brides have

    courted ;

In these deep vales the massive glaciers rested

Their mountain peaks, with polar snows yet

    crested,

While round their base the ocean currents drift-

    ing,

From nether depths these sandy hills were lifting.

Slowly they rose, slowly the waves retreated,

Like army huge in battle sore defeated,

Leaving the field with vengeance all unsated,

Still backward driven by the foeman hated.

Slow crept the grass o'er land from ocean

    wrested,

And in green robe this sea-born child invested,

Till shrub, and flower, and stately forest tree

Waved palms victorious o'er the conquered sea,

Which oft in madness fought for its own again,

Its columns charging o'er yonder wide moraine.

But vain the struggle; each wave and current
     bore

Some ocean tribute to the conquering shore.

Dense forests waved where, in the century old,

A shoreless ocean its crested billows rolled.

The oaks grew sturdy where once sea monsters
     strayed,

And foxes burrowed where erst the cod-fish
     played.

Then came the red man, closely following here

The weary wanderings of the hunted deer.

Ofttimes, mayhap, he stood upon this sandy hill,

On summer eve when the winds and waves were
     still.

Oft when the storm upon the wave came dashing,

His wigwam shuddered at the breaker's crashing.

The paleface came.   The moccasin now no
  more
Leaves its light impress on this smooth sandy
  shore.
Huge ocean steamers press yonder waves that
  knew
No heavier burden than the light birch canoe ;
Forests have fallen — the Indian passed away,
These hills themselves seem sore stricken by
  decay ;
Old ocean fretteth for that soon coming hour,
When time shall yield it back its ancient dower,
Its billows revelling in their old domain,
And its breakers dashing o'er these hills again.
Well, be it so — 'twill not disturb our sleeping,
If o'er our grave the ocean wave is sweeping.
The spirit freed, its earthly fetters spurning,
Back to its chains will know no sad returning.

Clothed in its angel robes, will it turn to earth,

To seek the shredded garments of its lower birth?

Safe, its palace reached, will e'er the soul com-
plain,

The ruined hut it left is whelmed beneath the
main?

What matter, then, if 'neath bright flowers we
rest,

Or the billows bloom above with their snowy
crest?

The spirit marching on, knows no backward
tread,

Marching with the living — not mouldering with
the dead.

GOOD-BY.

BROTHER, toiling where the Master
   Has to thee thy post assigned ;
Sister, well the picture filling
   By the Father's hand designed —

If in your heart, amid your toiling,
   I have waked a happy thought ;
If to you, when tears were falling,
   I some ray of joy have brought ;

If for you, now far off dwelling,
   My rude song to memory
Has lent some picture, brightly telling
   Of a cottage by the sea —

When thy mother's face was gladness,

    When thy father's arm was strong,

When there was no look of sadness

    In the gleeful fireside throng —

When thy locks were bright and sunny,

    As is still thy native sand,

When thy treasures were but sea shells,

    Gathered on the ocean strand;

If like music far off swelling,

    Over wood and valley long,

Comes Atlantic's deep bass, breathing

    As of old thy cradle song —

Then my song, though rough and lowly,

    Still to thee is not in vain,

For it wakens music holy,

    In thy weary soul again.

Thus we part, like good ships sailing

'Neath an ever foggy sky:

Scarcely ended is our hailing,

Ere 's exchanged a long good-by.

And may we, though singly drifting

Toward the dark and moaning sea,

Gladly mark, when clouds are lifting,

The destined harbor — *well alee.*